"Guess you are in the race horse business," Steve said with a grin. He wouldn't have been disturbed much if the top blew off of old Crystal Mountain.

"I can do it, Pop," Ben said desperately. "I can break this horse and pay Uncle Wes. I know I can, if you'll just give me a chance." He did his best to sound convincing.

Vince held a stirrup and put his foot in it. "It looks like you'll have to," he said slowly. He swung up. "You've made a deal, and it's up to you to keep it. I hope you can do it. But"—he reined his horse back to add—"watch yourself with that horse. Don't take any fool chances."

# The Midnight Colt

## GLENN BALCH

AVON BOOKS
*An Imprint of* HarperCollins*Publishers*

*To Elizabeth R.*
*whose fine work on this and*
*other books has contributed*
*splendidly to young America's reading*

The Midnight Colt

Copyright © 1952 by Glenn Balch

Published by arrangement with Thomas Y. Crowell Company.

www.harperchildrens.com

Library of Congress Cataloging-in-Publication Data

Balch, Glenn.

The midnight colt / Glenn Balch.—1st Avon ed.

p.   cm.

Summary: When Ben and his younger sister Dixie acquire Peck, the skittish, high-strung
racehorse that everyone seems to have given up on, they are convinced that, with patience
and care, they can retrain him to be a winner on the track.

ISBN 0-06-056367-2 (pbk.)   —   ISBN 0-06-056368-0 (lib. bdg.)

[1. Horses—Juvenile fiction. [Horses—Fiction. 2. Brothers and sisters—Fiction.
3. Ranch life—Idaho—Fiction. 4. Idaho—History—20th century—Fiction.] I. Title.

PZ10.3B183Mi  2004                                                      2003069101

[Fic]—dc22                                                                  CIP

                                                                             AC

First Avon edition, 2004

AVON TRADEMARK REG. U.S. PAT. OFF. AND IN OTHER COUNTRIES,

MARCA REGISTRADA, HECHO EN U.S.A.

Typography by Amy Ryan

❖

Visit us on the World Wide Web!

www.harperchildrens.com

# ◄•*One*•►

ars were gathering that bright Saturday afternoon at the big fairground on the outskirts of
Boise. They came in steady streams, out Fairview and
Irving and Emerald streets, turned in through the big
gates, and nosed into orderly rows in the parking areas.
Across the green infield of the half-mile oval track flags
and bunting fluttered gaily above the big concrete
grandstand. People trickled steadily into the rows of
sun-washed seats.

"Wow," said Dixie Darby, as she got out of the car,
"look at all the people."

"They like horse races, just like they do rodeos,"
Uncle Wes said.

"They're not as exciting," Ben said. He was Dixie's

brother, two years older and with yellow hair two shades darker. The eyes of both of them were blue, and Dixie had a sprinkling of freckles across the bridge of her nose. They were in Boise from the Darby ranch for the school term and stayed with Uncle Wes and Aunt Mary.

"Maybe that's a matter of opinion," Uncle Wes said. "I've seen some mighty interesting horse races." Uncle Wes was a round little man who wore thick glasses and worked in a Boise bank. He liked horses and prided himself on his knowledge of them, though actually most of his experience had been as a spectator and not as a rider.

Ben and Dixie, on the other hand, had ridden Tack Ranch horses all their lives and Ben, although too polite to say so, was not much impressed by Uncle Wes's show of knowledge. He realized too that Uncle Wes, in his rambling talk, meant only the best.

"And there's big money in race horses, too," Uncle Wes went on. "You'd be surprised, Ben. I've seen the checks."

Ben nodded, remembering that Uncle Wes worked in a bank, where he would have ample opportunity to know such things.

With Aunt Mary, who was their mother's sister,

they made their way through the crowd toward the grandstand entrance.

"Yes, sir," Uncle Wes said, "almost any kind of a race horse will bring in a thousand dollars. I wouldn't mind owning one."

"What would you do with a race horse—or any other kind?" Aunt Mary asked him.

A thousand dollars! Ben found himself resenting the amount. They weren't worth it, he thought angrily. Why, two hundred and fifty dollars was a fair price for a plumb good saddle horse. And saddle horses, being animals that a rancher could do work on, had real value. Of course he knew he might get a thousand dollars for Inky, his prized roping horse, but Inky, having won the Western Idaho state roping contest under Johnny Horn, was a horse in a thousand and moreover was not for sale at any price. Race horses were just for show. Ben had heard his father say that he wouldn't have one on the ranch, that he didn't have feed for a horse that couldn't do an honest day's work with cattle. That was the way Ben felt about it too. But a thousand dollars was a shocking amount of money.

At the grandstand entrance Uncle Wes, tickets in hand, halted and turned to them. "Say," he said, "these tickets are for reserved seats and it's thirty minutes till the races start. How'd you like to go back to the barns for a look at the horses first?"

"I'd like that," Dixie said. "I'd just like to see what a thousand-dollar horse looks like." Though they had seen many rodeos, this was the first time either she or Ben had ever attended a race meet. The closest they had been to racing was running the wild horses in Twin Buttes.

"Me too," Ben said.

All four of them went on to the stables, Uncle Wes leading the way importantly. The first stalls they came to were in the form of a big *U*, and the ranch-raised Darby children were at once engrossed in the activity and color of the scene. Horses were everywhere, in the stalls, in the area, and moving back and forth. Some were blanketed, others were being groomed, and still others were being walked or ridden about in small circles. Men, obviously trainers, grooms, and riders, mingled with the horses. There was the rich odor of dust and sweat and manure; there was the hoarse cajoling of voices and the tap of a hammer tightening a shoe. Other spectators, men and women in sport shirts almost as colorful as the jockeys' silks, strolled here and there.

The horses drew Ben Darby's eyes like magnets. Any horse was an object of interest for him, and these were easy to look at. He immediately recognized the thoroughbred characteristics: the high lean withers, the slender necks, the long smooth backs, and slim fine-boned legs. He noticed the big bright eyes and the trim restless ears. He had to admit that they were good-looking, but not a thousand dollars worth. Only ability could equal a thousand dollars in his practical mind.

"Gee," Dixie murmured admiringly. She was looking at a bright sorrel whose deep, flat hips glinted in the sun like polished brass.

"Nice horse," Ben agreed, being careful not to sound too enthusiastic. "But I like 'em shorter in the back."

"There's a beauty," Uncle Wes said, nodding. This horse was a dark bay, with a white spot marking his shapely head.

"Yeah," Ben said. "I bet he'd stampede right through a bunch of cattle, though."

"He shows speed," Uncle Wes said. "Look at those legs."

Ben was forced to admit it. "He sure does," he said. "Somebody has done a lot of work on these horses.

Look how slick their coats are. I'll bet they've been blanketed in a barn all winter." He thought then about the wintering conditions of the wild horses which he and Dixie had seen only a few months before and added, "They wouldn't last long in the Owyhee breaks."

"No," Dixie said, her face sobered by the recollection, "but no horse should have to go through that."

"That's right," Ben answered, "but I like horses that can if they have to. I like them strong and tough, like King." King was the black leader of the biggest of the Twin Buttes wild bunches.

"Don't forget King's a thoroughbred, like these," Dixie pointed out.

"Sure he is," Uncle Wes said, remembering the wild stallion's history.

"Yes, but he is wild-raised," Ben said. "That makes a difference. Out there in the rocks and brush they learn things these horses will never know."

They moved on slowly, watching the horses and their handlers. Long accustomed to people, most of the horses still in their stalls drowsed indifferently. Suddenly Ben halted, so abruptly that Dixie said, "What is it? What's the matter?"

Ben was looking at the head and neck of a brown

horse, a horse still in one of the stalls. Little wrinkles came to the corners of his eyes and he said, "That horse looks familiar. I think I've seen him somewhere before, or one mighty like him."

Dixie looked at the horse and shook her head. "I don't remember him. Where'd you see him?"

Ben was visibly puzzled. "I don't know," he said. "There's something about his head, something about his head and neck . . ." He moved closer to the stall and Dixie followed him. "Watch him," Ben cautioned. "He's a stallion." The horse showed no signs of mean-ness and Ben fastened a hand firmly in the noseband of his halter.

"He's all right," Dixie said.

"Seems to be," Ben said. "But I don't know if you can trust these race stallions." Nevertheless, still keep-ing a firm grip on the halter, he leaned into the stall, first on one side of the horse and then the other. "No brand," he announced presently. "Wait a minute. Here's something on his shoulder. I can't tell what it is; looks like a half circle or something."

"Maybe it's just an old hurt scar," Dixie said. "Andy Blair said they don't usually brand race horses." Andy Blair was the owner of an Arizona racing stud who had visited Tack in search of a lost colt.

"If it's a brand, it's not much of a job," Ben said. He turned the halter loose and stepped back to look at the horse's trim head again, this time from a front view.

"Like that one?" Uncle Wes asked cheerfully, coming up with Aunt Mary.

"He's not bad," Ben said. "I thought at first I knew him. There's something about him that I seem to remember."

Dixie turned to a man standing nearby, a man who by his clothes and manner appeared to be a trainer or an owner. "Is this your horse, mister?" she asked.

The man shook his head. "No, he belongs to Dabney Clouse." He looked around. "I don't see Dabney now. He was here a little while ago. He's not entered till the fifth."

"Where'd he come from?" Ben asked, nodding at the horse. "Do you know anything about him?"

"Oregon, I think," the man said. "Some place near Pendleton, as I remember. You know him?"

Ben hesitated, then shook his head. "No, I guess not. At first I thought I might. Do you know his name?"

"Peck," the man said.

"Peck?" Dixie repeated, frowning.

The man nodded. "That's what Dabney calls him."

"Do you know anything about his breeding?" Ben asked.

"He's hot blood," the man said. Then, after a glance at them, he added, "Thoroughbred."

"What's his sire? Do you know?" Ben asked.

The man shook his head. "I couldn't tell you. Dabney ought to be back soon. He'll know. He can tell you everything about him."

Uncle Wes had been listening and now, thinking to make a point with Ben, he said, "There's one thing I'd like to know: how much is a horse like that worth? How much will he bring, if you can tell me, mister?"

The man's eyes widened and he hesitated briefly. "Well," he said, "it all depends. Are you interested in buying a horse—a race horse?"

"I might be," Uncle Wes said, nodding his head as though he meant it. "I might be interested in a good race horse, if the price is right."

Ben and Dixie kept straight faces, but Ben saw Aunt Mary punch Uncle Wes in the ribs from behind with her thumb. Uncle Wes's seriousness didn't change however.

"Dabney might sell him," the man said. "I happen to know that. He's got a nice two-year-old coming along that he wants to give his attention to, so I'm pretty sure he would sell this horse. He's a good one, four years old and as sound as a singletree. You wouldn't go wrong on him."

"Can he run?" Dixie asked shrewdly.

"Sure," the man said. "Course he can. He's a race horse. Don't he look it?"

"How much is the price?" Uncle Wes said.

"Well, I couldn't say for sure," the man said. "He's not my horse. You'll have to see Dabney. But I figure he would be a good buy at around a thousand. I don't think you can get him for any less."

"A thousand dollars?" Uncle Wes repeated, giving Ben a see-I-told-you-so glance.

"Yes, a thousand dollars," the man said. "I think maybe Dabney will sell him for that. You want me to check it for you? I'll go find Dabney."

Uncle Wes considered the matter with a serious expression, then said, "No, not right now. I'll think about it. I've got a couple more good-looking horses in mind. If I decide I'm interested, I'll come back."

"If you want him at that price, you'd better buy him

before his race," the man said. "If he wins, there'll be plenty after him. The price will go up. Now's the time to talk to Dabney."

"Come on, Wes," Aunt Mary said, twitching at his sleeve. "It's time for the races to start."

"He's a good-looking horse," Uncle Wes said to the man as he permitted Aunt Mary to lead him away. "I might be back."

Ben and Dixie followed, and as soon as they were out of hearing Aunt Mary said, "You know you can't just go off and buy yourself a horse, Wes. The very thought!"

"Now who's to say I can't?" Uncle Wes teased her gently. "I might. I would just kind of like to have a good race horse. I've got the money too."

"Yes," said Aunt Mary, "but what do you think horses eat—canceled checks? I suppose we could stable it in the spare bedroom, after Dixie goes back to the ranch."

Ben grinned and said, "You can put him down in the basement with me, if he can get up and down the stairs."

"That's right," Uncle Wes said, "make fun. Well, I might fool you. I just might . . ."

## ◄•*Two*•►

**B**en and Dixie found the races more exciting than they had expected. The lean long-legged thoroughbreds were not the type of horses they were accustomed to at their father's Tack Ranch, but they were quick to realize the tremendous heart and gameness of the animals as they battled it out neck and neck around the track. Ben's admiration went out to each winner as it came, giving the best in its finely trained body, down the stretch to the finish. This racing business, he was soon forced to admit, called for a "lot of horse," as the range riders sometimes expressed it.

And Dixie was even more impressed. "Isn't that bay a beauty?" she said, when the horses paraded in front of the stands before the third race.

"He's a nice-looking horse," Ben said.

"Look at that springy action," Dixie said. "I bet he wins."

Ben shook his head. "That big sorrel'll beat him."

"Don't be too sure of that," Uncle Wes said. "Cal Spurgeon is riding that bay."

"What's that got to do with it?" Ben asked.

"Plenty," Uncle Wes said. "Cal Spurgeon is the best jockey around here."

"A horse can only run so fast," Ben said.

"Yes, but the jockey can be a big help to him," Uncle Wes said. "He can save his strength for when it counts. He can tell him how to run and when to turn on the steam. He can keep him from getting boxed by the others, and keep him from running on the outside all the way around. A horse that runs on the outside has farther to go than one that stays on the rail. Did you know that?"

"Yes, sir," Ben said. "But isn't it mostly luck?"

"Not any more than in a roping contest," Uncle Wes said. "Do you think it was just luck Inky won?"

"No, but roping takes a real rider," Ben said.

"So does racing," Uncle Wes said. "These boys are experts. A smart rider can mean the difference between two evenly matched horses."

"I bet Gaucho would make a good jockey," Dixie said. "He can handle horses better than anybody I know. They'll do anything for him."

"I wouldn't say so," Uncle Wes said, with a dubious shake of his head. "He seems pretty big to me. How much does he weigh?"

"Not as much as I do," Ben said. "He doesn't weigh over one hundred and forty."

"Too much," Uncle Wes said. "You know what those jockeys out there weigh?"

"No," Ben said.

"Guess," Uncle Wes said.

"I don't know," Ben said. "They don't look very big. Most of them look like they were just boys."

"One hundred pounds," said Uncle Wes, "or not more than one hundred and ten. With their saddles and everything, they're between one hundred and twenty and a hundred and thirty. And they're not just boys; most of them are grown men. Weight is mighty important in a horse race. Even a single pound counts when a horse has to carry it at top speed for a mile. Gaucho would be too heavy."

"Then, I guess I would be too," Ben said. He'd

14

secretly been comparing himself with the riders out on the track.

Uncle Wes nodded. "You're not built for it. But this Cal Spurgeon is a natural. He's grown, better than twenty years old, but he's little and dried up. He doesn't weigh much more than a hundred pounds, and he's got plenty of nerve. It takes nerve, too. A jockey's got to have confidence in his horse and be willing to take a chance."

"Gaucho has plenty of nerve," Dixie said. "You should see him head out through the brush at a dead run. He'll ride a horse anywhere."

"That's one kind of riding," Uncle Wes said, "but this is another kind. Oh, I'm not saying," he went on, knowing well enough how much Ben and Dixie admired their father's horse trainer, "that Gaucho can't ride. He's just too heavy for track riding, that's all. If he was down to a hundred pounds—"

"They're ready to start," Aunt Mary said. "They're lining up."

The horses were started from a line instead of from a gate such as is often used on the important tracks and in big races. Their riders were trying to keep them abreast of each other in accordance with the starter's commands, yet at the same time each jockey was covertly working for and hoping for an advantage. Each wanted to have his mount collected, ready to spring forward, and just as much to the front as possible. All the horses felt the tension and knew what was coming, that at any instant the jockeys would be crying wildly in their ears and digging at their ribs with their heels. The horses couldn't stay still. They twisted and turned; they took their bits in their teeth and broke from the line, only to be sawed to a halt and brought back. And the longer the starting required, the more nervous they became.

"They ought to use the starting gate," Uncle Wes said. "That's best."

"What's a starting gate?" Dixie asked, without taking her eyes from the nervous horses.

"It's a row of narrow stalls, each one with a gate in front," Uncle Wes explained. "They get the horses in the stalls, then the starter pulls a lever and all the gates fly open at the same time. That way, every horse gets an even chance."

"There they go!" Aunt Mary cried. "They're off!"

There were five horses in the race, and they got away in a bunch, the big sorrel that Ben thought likely to win out in front. The sorrel's rider took him at once to the rail and kept him there, causing Ben to realize that here was a smart jockey, too. At the first turn the bunch began to loosen. Ben saw that there were three horses on the rail and two running beyond these three, on the outside. The bay that had attracted Dixie's attention was the third horse back, behind the sorrel and a second bay.

They held this position around the second turn and into the back stretch. Here one of the outside horses began to come up, and Ben could see that the rider was using his stick. The horse gained until he was neck and neck with the big sorrel, then the sorrel lengthened his stride and the outside horse could not gain any more. The second outside horse dropped behind, but the three horses on the rail still ran close together. They went into the far turn in this manner, and Ben saw that the extra distance was beginning to tell on the first outside horse, for it faltered and began to lose ground. The horses swept around the far end of the track and came into the stretch. Ben could see their bobbing heads, could see the jockeys lying well forward along their necks. The big sorrel was still in the lead, but he swung a bit wide in making the turn, leaving a gap at the rail. Almost instantly that gap was filled, by a bay. How it got there, Ben couldn't tell, but it was the trim bay Dixie had noticed. It forged ahead with a fine burst of speed, and pulled up with the sorrel. For a few seconds, while the crowd shouted and yelled with excitement, the two horses ran even. Then the bay gained still more and came on to win by half a length.

Dixie was on her feet and yelling. "Good horse, good horse," she cried. "There! What'd I tell you, Ben?"

"He is a good horse," Ben said. "And it was a honey of a race."

"And he got a honey of a ride," Uncle Wes said. "Did you see Cal Spurgeon bring him through on the rail?"

"I sure did," Ben said, nodding his head. "I see what you mean, Uncle Wes."

The fourth race, for three-eighths of a mile, was not as good as the third, but Ben's interest picked up again when the horses came out for the fifth race. "Say," he said, "there's that Peck horse."

"Who?" Dixie asked.

"Peck," Ben said. "The horse we were looking at at the stables. See him? His jockey is wearing a green cap."

"I see him," Dixie said.

"He's a good horse," Ben said. "There's something about him I like."

"He's a big horse," Uncle Wes said.

"His legs are not as trim as that bay's," Dixie said.

"No, but he's got a lot of heart and a lot of lung room," Ben said.

"He's sure wild," Aunt Mary said. "I don't think I want him in my bedroom."

The big brown was rearing and plunging. He suddenly took the bit in his teeth and ran fifty yards before his rider could stop him.

"He's a bad actor," Uncle Wes said. "That jockey is having a time with him." Uncle Wes had obviously forgotten his threat to buy the animal.

As the jockey turned the horse to bring him back to the starting line, Ben saw that the animal was already wringing wet with sweat. "He's nervous," Ben said. "He's excited."

"He sure is," Uncle Wes said.

The horse, now back in the starting line, suddenly reared.

"Oh," Aunt Mary cried, "he's going to fall over backward."

And for a second Ben thought she was right, for the horse was standing almost perpendicular. But he came down to the front, his feet hitting the earth with a jar that almost unseated the jockey. The jockey saved himself from falling only by grabbing around the horse's neck.

Uncle Wes shook his head and said, "He can't handle that horse."

"He's afraid of him," Ben guessed.

"Who wouldn't be?" Aunt Mary asked.

The exasperated starter was now talking to the rider on the brown horse sternly, telling him to get in line and stay there. But the horse still reared and plunged.

"He sure is a wild one," Uncle Wes said, grinning at Ben. "He acts like he was right off of Twin Buttes."

Twin Buttes was wild-horse country, back of Tack Ranch in the rugged Owyhees, where Ben and Dixie loved to watch the stallions and their bands. It was stern and harsh land, high and rocky, growing mostly brush and scrub juniper, but the hardy wild horses thrived on it.

"Yes," Ben said. Then suddenly his eyes became bright and he almost got to his feet. "Say," he said. "Say, Dix, I know now."

"Know what? What is it?" she asked.

"Say," Ben said. "Look at that horse. Look at his head and neck. Does it remind you of—of anything?"

Dixie looked and searched her memory, then said, "No, not that I can think of, Ben. Why?"

"Oh—nothing," Ben said. "I just thought maybe it would."

Dixie turned back to the track. "I can't understand it," she said. "He didn't act crazy like that in his stall."

"That's the trouble with these race horses," Uncle Wes said knowingly. "They haven't got any sense when they get excited. You can't do a thing with them."

That agreed with Ben's idea about ranchers having no use for race horses. After a season or two on the race tracks, they were much too nervous and excitable for use in working cattle. Speed was all right, but it was no good in range country unless it could be controlled. A man working cattle would be better off on foot.

"He's crazy as a galoot," Uncle Wes said.

Ben didn't answer. He just shook his head. The brown horse wasn't crazy. Ben was sure of that. Horses, he felt, were much more stable mentally than people and none were ever crazy, except of course after suffering a bad accident, or eating locoweed, or something like that.

But there did seem to be something the matter with this big brown horse. He reared and plunged, and backed and turned. He pawed and tossed his head. He twisted and turned, bumping recklessly into the other horses and increasing their excitement. His rider was fast losing control of him. A man in a brown wind-breaker ran out on the track, grabbed the horse's bridle, and managed after much tugging to get him up to the starting line. But he couldn't hold him there. The horse reared and lunged, narrowly missing the man with his front feet. He broke free and bolted along the track. The jockey sawed angrily at the bit, but the horse had rounded the first turn before he could be halted.

"Bring out the gate," someone in the stands shouted. "Where's the starting gate?"

"He won't go in a gate either," another man, sitting nearby, said. "Take him off," he yelled. "Let's get this race started."

The starter spoke sternly to the man in the wind-breaker. The man grabbed the horse's reins with both hands and swung him around into the starting line. The jockeys brought the other horses up, and for a second it looked as if there might be a start. Then the quivering, sweat-drenched brown horse reared again. Dragging the man with him, he slammed into the horse on his left and the whole group was in hopeless confusion.

The people in the stands groaned unhappily at the delay.

The starter shouted something to the man hanging to the brown horse and made a crisp gesture toward the gate with his thumb.

"He's sending him to the barns," Uncle Wes said.

"What?" Dixie asked.

"He's ruling him off the track," Uncle Wes explained. "They do that with horses that won't start."

"He won't get to run?" Ben asked disappointedly.

"No," Uncle Wes said. "It probably doesn't make any difference; he's worn out already."

The jockey dismounted and slapped his boot leg angrily with his whip. Hot words passed between him and the man in the windbreaker. The man led the horse along the track and out the gate, which another man firmly closed behind him.

"They're off!" Aunt Mary cried.

Ben brought his eyes back to the running horses, but he wasn't very much interested. He hardly noticed which one came in first. He couldn't get the picture of that sweat-dripping brown horse out of his mind. Presently he got to his feet.

"Wait a minute, Ben," Uncle Wes said. "There's another race."

"I know it," Ben said, but began moving toward the aisle.

"Where're you going?" Aunt Mary asked.

"I want to see something," Ben said. "I'll be back. If I'm not, I'll meet you at the car when it's over."

Dixie looked up at Ben narrowly and said, "What's the matter?"

"Nothing," Ben said. "Can't a guy even go to the bathroom?"

# ◄• *Three* •►

*L*eaving the grandstand, Ben Darby went immedi- ately to the big *U*-shaped stables. He was a lean youth, with a good-boned frame and a wind-tanned face. The stall which the brown horse had occupied was empty, so Ben moved on to the cooling area, where men and boys were leading blanketed horses in slow varying circles.

The excitement of the running over, the horses now moved with weary indifference. Ben found the man in the brown windbreaker. The horse he led bore so little resemblance to the rearing, plunging creature that had been on the track that Ben looked carefully at the trim head to be certain it was the same animal. The man's eyes were downcast and the expression on his face was one of deep discouragement. Even the horse seemed to share it.

Ben fell in step beside the man and asked, "What happened to him? Why wouldn't he start?"

The man looked up, without welcome or any trace of friendliness. "You tell me," he said shortly.

"He's been mishandled," Ben said. "Somebody made a mistake with him."

"Yeah," the man said, with some sarcasm. "What do you know about horses?"

"I've worked a few," Ben said. "I own a couple."

The man looked at him and said, "I suppose you think you could handle this one?"

Ben nodded and said, "I think I could. But I wanted to ask you about him."

"You can have the chance," the man said sullenly. "I'll sell him to you cheap."

"Who's his sire? What's he out of?" Ben asked.

"What difference does it make?" the man said. "He's purebred. I'll guarantee the papers."

Ben was not surprised to see a slim girl in a blue dress walking across the area toward them. He knew he had not fooled his sister in the grandstand. Dixie seemed to have some strange ability to read his mind at times.

"Are you Dabney Clouse? Do you own him?" he asked the man.

"Yes," the man said, stopping to face Ben. "Do you want to buy him? Put up or shut up, if you think you're so good. He's yours for five hundred dollars, son, not a cent less."

Ben shook his head. "I wouldn't give more than three hundred," he said. "He's—"

"Sold," Dabney Clouse said. He handed the lead rope to Ben. "He's your horse. I'll throw in the halter and blanket."

"But—" Ben said, his mouth hanging somewhat helplessly open.

"What's this?" Dixie said, coming up.

"This young man just bought a horse," Dabney Clouse informed her.

"Bought a horse?" Dixie cried. "You, Ben?"

"Yes, sir," Dabney Clouse said. "He came here and made his brag. Said he could cure this horse."

"Did you, Ben?" Dixie asked.

"I said I thought I could," Ben said. "I'd like the chance."

"You've got it," the man said. "What's your name?"

"Ben Darby," Ben said. The big horse moved a step

forward, sniffed Ben's hand, and then rubbed his soft dark nose against it.

"But—" Dixie said. "Did you actually buy him, Ben? Did you?" She rubbed the horse's nose.

"Well—I— He said he wouldn't take less than five hundred dollars, Dix," he said.

"Five hundred dollars!" Dixie said, her blue eyes becoming big and round.

"I just offered him three hundred," Ben said.

"What did he say then?"

"He took me up on it," Ben said.

"Gee, Ben. Three hundred dollars," Dixie said.

"Of course, if you haven't got the money I guess the deal is off," Dabney Clouse said. "Also I don't guess I could sell a horse to anyone as young as you are." He held out his hand for the lead rope and the corners of his eyes crinkled in the suggestion of a grin.

But something seemed to make it impossible for Ben to give that rope back. Something had happened to him in those few minutes; maybe it was the way the brown horse had rubbed his hand. "Wait a minute," he said to Dabney Clouse.

"I've got about twenty dollars," Dixie said. "Maybe we could get some money from Pop."

Ben shook his head. "Pop hasn't much use for race horses," he said.

"I guess I'll just have to take him back," Dabney Clouse said, reaching again for the lead rope.

"No," Ben said. "Dix, go get Uncle Wes."

Dixie turned and hurried toward the grandstand.

"Who's Uncle Wes?" Dabney Clouse asked.

"He's a banker," Ben said. "I think he'll let me have the money."

"Are you serious about this, boy?" Dabney Clouse said.

"Yes, sir," Ben said, nodding his head.

Uncle Wes and Dixie arrived, with Aunt Mary trailing behind. When informed of the deal, Uncle Wes became slightly flustered.

"Please loan me the money," Ben said. "I'll pay you back."

"Yes, sir," Dixie said. "We'll pay you back, Uncle Wes."

"But—but—" Uncle Wes said. "Three hundred dollars is a lot of money, an awful lot."

"We'll pay you interest," Dixie said. "We'll pay you back with interest."

"Six percent?" Uncle Wes asked.

"Yes, sir," Ben said, "six percent. Three hundred dollars is not much for a good race horse. You said so yourself, Uncle Wes. Remember?"

"Yes, but—what'll your father say?" Uncle Wes asked.

"He's not in this," Ben said. "This is strictly a business deal between us, Uncle Wes."

"He's a dandy horse," Dixie said.

"Well," Uncle Wes said, "if I make you this loan, how do you plan to repay it?"

"Why, I—" Ben began, not certain.

"When we sell the horse," Dixie said. "We'll pay the money back when we sell the horse."

"But how do you know you can sell him?" Uncle Wes said. "From what I just saw out on the track, I'm not sure anybody will want him."

"He's not always that bad," Dabney Clouse said.

"They will," Dixie declared enthusiastically. "When we get him trained, they'll want him."

"I'm going to work him," Ben said.

"I paid fifteen hundred for him, less than six months ago," Dabney Clouse said.

"But what I want to know," Uncle Wes said, paying no attention to Dabney Clouse, "is what happens if you can't sell him? Suppose nobody wants him? What happens if Ben can't break him of rearing and plunging like that? No one will have him."

This stumped Dixie. "Why—" she said. "But Ben can train him. I'm sure he can."

"I'll pay you back, Uncle Wes," Ben promised seriously. "No matter what happens, I'll see that you get your money back."

"But how?" Uncle Wes asked. "I just want to know how you'll do it. This race horse business is mighty tricky, I tell you."

"Why not let them have it, Wes? The experience in business will be good for them," Aunt Mary urged.

"I know it's tricky," Ben said. "But I'll pay you back, Uncle Wes. I'll pay you back, even if I have to sell my roping horse. You know there's half a dozen fellows who would jump at a chance to buy Inky. You know that."

"But, Ben," Dixie cried, "Inky's your 'Christmas horse.' You couldn't sell him."

"I will if I have to," Ben said, nodding his head. "If I can't break this horse to start races, I'll sell Inky to pay Uncle Wes."

Uncle Wes knew what the black roping horse meant

to Ben. He was silent a few seconds, then he said, "All right, you can have the money. I'll write Mr. Clouse a check and you can close the deal. Monday I'll get a blank note from the bank, and you and Dixie can sign it, just to make it legal."

"Fine," Dixie said. "We'll do it, Uncle Wes."

"Who'll I make the bill of sale to?" Dabney Clouse asked. "It ought to be to a grown person. In some states it might not be legal to a person under age."

"Why," Uncle Wes said. "Why," he went on, pushing out his chest, "you can just make it to me. I guess I'm old enough to own a horse. That all right with you, Ben?"

"Sure is, Uncle Wes," Ben said.

"And don't forget he's half mine," Dixie said.

"Shucks," Uncle Wes said to Aunt Mary, "I almost wish I had bought him myself."

## ◄ • *Four* • ►

**B**en and Dixie Darby owned the race horse Peck before they discovered how little they really knew about him. They besieged Dabney Clouse with questions while he was pocketing Uncle Wes's check. Clouse had bought the horse in Oregon, from a man who had had him only a short time. He didn't know where he was raised, but thought it was probably some place around Pendleton. His papers showed that he was out of a mare by the name of Miss Peck and sired by a horse called Big Trouble.

"I guess that's how he came by his name, Peck o' Trouble," Dabney told them.

"Ouch," Dixie said. "Couldn't they think of something better than that?"

Dabney grinned and said, "That's his registered name. But you can just call him Peck. Or Brownie, if you like that better. But of course if you enter him in a race, you'll have to enter him by his full name."

"His name doesn't worry me," Ben said. "How long has he been acting like this, like he did on the track?"

"Ever since I've had him," Clouse said. "I don't know how long before. I had a boy I thought could ride him."

"Could he?" Dixie asked.

"He was up on him today," Clouse said. "You could see for yourself."

"Have you tried to break him of it?" Ben asked with interest.

"I've tried everything I know," the man said.

"Don't worry, Ben," Dixie said. "We'll cure him."

"Good luck," Dabney Clouse said. "And let me know how you did it." He turned and left them.

Uncle Wes had already gone with Aunt Mary back to the grandstand.

Ben looked at Dixie. Dixie looked back at Ben, and they both turned to look at the horse, which was standing quietly under his blanket at the end of the rope. "Well, we've got him," Dixie said, as if still hardly able to believe it. "Now we've got to find some place to keep him."

Ben nodded and said, "Let's go find the superintendent."

The superintendent agreed that they could keep Peck in one of the stalls temporarily. "But," he said, "you'll have to buy hay and grain, and look after him yourselves."

That satisfied Ben and Dixie. "That's what we want to do," Dixie said.

Ben found a man they could borrow bedding straw and feed from until they could have some sent out, and they fixed a stall for Peck and put him in it, carefully latching the door.

"Yes, sir," Dixie said, with a last look to make sure everything was all right before they went to find Uncle Wes and Aunt Mary, "we've got ourselves a running horse, Ben."

"We sure have," Ben agreed.

"But I'm wondering," Dixie went on thoughtfully, "what Pop is going to say."

"We won't tell him," Ben said, "not until we have to."

"It won't be long till school's out," Dixie said. "What then?"

"Maybe we'll have him sold by then," Ben said, hopefully.

"That would help," Dixie said.

The next day was Sunday, so all they did was feed and water the new horse. Uncle Wes drove them by on the way to Sunday School, and again in the afternoon.

Monday, after school, they put on their boots and riding clothes and asked Aunt Mary to drive them out to the fairground. She went on, to pick up Uncle Wes, and they would catch the bus back home.

The race meet was finished and most of the owners and jockeys and horses had moved on, leaving only a few stalls still occupied by locally owned horses and a few others kept there for training. Peck was dozing in the sunshine, his neck and big brown head out the window. "Hello, boy," Dixie called to him. He opened his eyes and turned his ears toward her. She went up to him and rubbed his nose gently.

"I'll get the halter rope," Ben said, "and we'll take him out, so I can clean his stall. Do you think you can lead him?"

"Sure," Dixie said.

"Well, watch him," Ben cautioned. "He may not be like our ranch horses."

"How's he different?" Dixie asked.

"He's been raised differently," Ben said. "He's probably been kept in a box stall all of his life, and there have always been people around him. He's not afraid of you and he may have learned some bad habits, like striking and biting. Remember he's a stallion."

"I will," Dixie said. "I'll keep an eye on him." She took the rope from Ben and said, "Come on." The horse followed her willingly enough. She led him in a circle in front of the stalls.

Ben watched a few minutes for any sign of stubbornness or meanness in the horse, then turned his attention to the stall. He forked the old bedding and manure through the window, raked the floor, and spread fresh bedding. He filled the water bucket and put it back in its rack in the corner.

"How's he doing?" he asked Dixie, after he'd finished.

She shrugged her shoulders in a slightly puzzled manner and said, "Fine. He's just as nice a horse as anybody could want. Look." She halted and the horse took an additional step so he could rub his nose in the middle of her back.

"Yes," Ben agreed. "Whoa, boy," he said and went to

the horse. Standing at Peck's shoulder, he reached down, caught the fetlock of a front foot and said, "Give it here." Peck lifted the foot readily and balanced on the other three legs while Ben examined it. Ben took up all four feet, one after another. "Good feet," he said. "And he's not cranky about them. New shoes, too."

"He's gentle," Dixie said. "I'd like to ride him."

Ben looked at the halter and rope, then shook his head. "Not without a bridle and saddle," he said.

"Maybe we could borrow one. We really ought to ride him, Ben."

Ben looked around. A stall near the corner was obviously serving as a tack room and the door was open. The owner was inside. He didn't have a stock saddle, which Ben would have preferred, but he did have a flat training saddle and a bridle with a light bar bit.

"Say," he said, "ain't you the kid who bought Dabney Clouse's horse?"

"Yes, sir," Ben said. "I'm going to get my saddle in from the ranch just as soon as I can."

"You're welcome to use this one," the man said. "But maybe you'd better take this bridle." He took another bridle down from the wall.

"Why?" Ben asked. He saw that the bridle was similar to the other one except that it had a strong curb bit.

"Oh, your horse might handle better in it," the man said.

"You think I'll need that stiff bit?" Ben asked, making it more of a statement than a question.

"You might," the man said.

"What do you know about Peck?" Ben said seriously.

"Nothing much," the man said. "He gets mighty nervous under a saddle. I saw him on the track last Saturday. If I was riding him, I'd use the curb."

"All right," Ben said.

Dixie wanted to ride the brown horse first, but Ben said, "No. Let me see how he acts first."

When the saddle was put on, the horse began to show some nervousness. Ben spoke to him quietly, cinched the saddle up firm, led him about in a small circle, and tested the cinch again. It was still tight.

"Want me to stand at his head?" Dixie asked.

Ordinarily Ben would have scorned this offer of assistance, but now he said, "Yes."

Peck pranced a bit as Ben swung up, but Dixie

stayed with the reins. Ben found the off stirrup, thrust his boot deep into it, and straightened up. The horse was noticeably nervous.

"All set?" Dixie asked.

Ben didn't feel secure in the strange flat saddle, and he certainly didn't want to get off to a bad start with this horse. "Lead him around in a circle," he said to Dixie.

She led the horse. Peck moved sideways, prancing. Ben expected him to calm down, but he didn't.

"What's the matter with him?" Dixie asked.

"I don't know," Ben said, shaking his head.

"Maybe he's not used to being led like this," Dixie said.

They made another circle, but the horse still swung wide, his front and hind feet making two separate sets of tracks. His neck was strongly arched against the pull of the rein in Dixie's hand.

"Think you can ride him?" Dixie asked.

Ben nodded and said, "Yes."

"Say when you're ready," Dixie said cheerfully.

Ben set his feet firmly in the stirrups and said, "Okay. Turn him loose."

Dixie let her hand drop, but kept walking with the

horse. Peck slowed uncertainly but moved on willingly enough when Ben clucked to him. He widened the circle.

"He's skittish," Dixie said, watching. "He wants to go."

"Yes," Ben said. "He's got plenty of spirit."

"Maybe too much," Dixie said.

"Not if it's handled right," Ben said. "I'm going to take him out on the track." He turned the horse out of the circle and away from the stables.

Dixie followed. As they approached the gate that was the entrance to the track, Peck's nervousness visibly increased. He began to toss his head and stretch his neck for more rein length. Ben reined him away from the gate and back toward the stables. Peck did not want to turn, but Ben was firm. Ben rode him in a circle for a few minutes, then halted him and rubbed his neck, which was already getting sticky with sweat.

"What's the matter, boy?" Ben said. "Take it easy. No one is going to hurt you. There's no use getting hot and bothered."

The horse seemed to calm down and Ben turned him back toward the gate. He fretted and pranced, but Ben rode him on and entered the track. Peck raised his head, looked about, and whinnied loudly. But the track was empty. Ben turned him to the left to face away from the direction races were run on the track. Peck began to prance and try to whirl back, first to one side and then the other. Ben gripped tightly with his knees to keep a firm seat in the slick saddle and insisted that the horse go ahead. Peck did, but unwillingly. Ben made him walk all the way around the track, and when they came back to the grandstand, where Dixie was perched on the railing, the horse was dripping sweat.

"Gee," Dixie said unhappily, "he's sure excited."

"Yep," Ben said, busy with the nervous horse.

"I guess he thinks there's going to be a race," Dixie said.

Ben nodded. He turned the horse in a small circle before the grandstand and was forced to keep a tight rein to keep him under control. He had ridden him about this circle several times when another horse and rider entered the track through the gate, which was a hundred yards or so away. Peck halted and threw up his head, watching this new horse. He paid no attention to Ben's heels against his ribs.

The strange rider, unaware of what was going on, turned his horse toward the grandstand and urged it to a gallop. Ben could feel a violent trembling in Peck as the other horse approached. The other horse had almost reached them when Peck whirled, took the bit in his teeth, and bolted. When Ben tried to pull him up, he reared and fought and plunged, causing Ben to feel more insecure than ever in the smooth, flat saddle.

Ben was gaining control of his horse when the strange rider, thinking the youth in front needed assistance, put his horse to a faster gait. Peck heard the pound of hoofs and after that there was only one thing on in his mind—run. He reared and plunged harder than ever, fighting with all his strength for his head.

"No, no," Ben said sternly, sawing at the reins.

He was making headway when the right stirrup leather broke loose from the flat saddle. Ben lurched to one side so violently that he nearly hit the ground. He saved himself by grabbing the horse's mane and finally succeeded in pulling himself back erect. By this time Peck was in full stride, running whether Ben liked it or not. Ben knew he had lost his first battle with the horse. He balanced himself as best he could with the one stirrup, tightened the reins, and said, "Whoa, Peck. Whoa."

But Peck had the bit in his teeth and kept on until

they flashed past the grandstand before he began to slow down. They were beyond the first turn before Ben succeeded in halting him. Ben turned him and rode back to the grandstand.

"Jeez, Ben," Dixie said from her seat on the railing. "He's worse than I thought. What happened?"

"Lost a stirrup," Ben panted, holding out his right foot for her to see. "He got away from me. When that other horse came in, he went crazy, Dix."

## ◄ • Five • ►

*B*en and Dixie Darby were quiet as they led the big
horse back to the stables. He was wringing wet
with sweat and they put the blanket on him to make
sure he didn't catch cold. They led him about, so he
would cool gradually, and after a time let him have a
few sips of water.

Dixie shook her head, a puzzled pucker between her
eyes. "I can't understand him, Ben," she said. "Look at
him. He's gentle as an old dog. But on a race track he
goes wild. Why?"

"It's the way he's been handled, I guess," Ben said.
"Somebody has made a fool of him."

"He gets so darned excited," Dixie said. "What are
we going to do about it?"

"Cure him," Ben said. "Come on, Peck." He resumed leading the horse.

Dixie walked at his side. "How?" she asked.

"Work on him," Ben said. "Enough work will bring any horse around."

"I don't know," Dixie said. "We never had one like this before. He's been spoiled. And Gaucho says a spoiled horse is a lot harder to train than one that has never had a saddle on his back."

Ben nodded. "That's right. I'd rather have one right off the range. A horse from the range doesn't know anything; a spoiled one knows too much. That's the trouble with Peck."

"What are we going to do about it?" Dixie asked. "How do you fix a horse that knows too much?"

"Make him forget it," Ben said. "Make him forget it, and then start training him all over again. And the second time, train him right."

"That's a big job, to make a horse forget," Dixie said.

"It can be done," Ben said.

"How?" Dixie asked.

"Well, in Peck's case, keep him away from race tracks," Ben said. "I made a mistake today, taking him out there. I'm going to keep him away from the track for a while."

"He'll need some exercise," Dixie said.

Ben nodded. "We'll lead him, and ride him in the exercise area behind the stables. Sure we'll keep working him, we just won't put him on the track. My idea is that he has been brought along too rapidly; he's had too much fast work, too much racing."

"That could be," Dixie said in agreement.

"Horses are not all alike," Ben went on, "but some people don't realize it. Peck's unusually high spirited. He's got an ornery stubborn streak in him, like King."

"Like King?" Dixie asked. "What do you mean?"

"King's that way," Ben said. "Don't you remember how he fought the ropes the time we caught him? He wouldn't give up; that's the reason Gaucho said the best thing to do was turn him loose again. He might have killed himself."

"But King is a wild horse," Dixie said.

"Peck's got a stubborn wild streak in him too," Ben said. "I could feel it, when he bolted out there on the track. He was going to run if it killed him."

"Well, we've got to get that out of him," Dixie said, "or he won't ever be any good."

"We will," Ben said. "We've got to work him slow and keep him away from the track for a while. It's going to take time."

"How much time?" Dixie asked.

"Two or three weeks probably," Ben said. "It's hard to tell."

"Well, I hope it doesn't take any longer," Dixie said. "It's only a little more than a month till school will be out."

Ben stopped again at the watering trough, to permit the horse to drink some more. "There," he said. "That's enough for now." He pulled Peck away from the trough and resumed leading him.

"Do you think we can have him sold by then?" Dixie said.

"I don't know," Ben said truthfully. "It's not very long."

"If we can't, what are we going to do?" Dixie asked.

Ben considered that and said, "I guess we'll have to take him out to Tack, if Pop'll let us."

"Oh, he'll let us," Dixie said. "But he may not be very happy about it. You know how he feels about race horses."

"Yes," Ben said.

"And he might not think we were very smart," Dixie went on.

"He won't," Ben said with certainty. "Jeez, Dix, three hundred dollars is a lot of money," he went on, as if he'd just realized it.

"It is—when you owe it," Dixie agreed. "What we've got to do, if we can, is to get Peck broken in and sell him before school is out. Then Pop needn't know, unless we want to tell him."

"Yep," Ben nodded, "that's the plan."

Having arrived at this conclusion, Ben and Dixie got to work. Every afternoon, as soon as possible after school, they went to the fairground to work the horse. And on Saturdays they spent the mornings there as well as the afternoons. They led Peck and rode him, then led him some more. They handled him as carefully as possible, doing nothing to excite him and keeping him away from the race track. But even then Ben found that he could not stay long on the horse's back before he began to tremble and sweat, to prance and fret and feel for the bit with his teeth. This in turn would lead to rearing and plunging, if Ben did not dismount.

After ten days and very little, if any, improvement,

Ben was discouraged. "I never saw a horse so crazy to run," he told Dixie. "That's all he can think about, when there's a saddle on his back."

"He's better," Dixie said, nodding her yellow head positively. "He's not as bad as he was. That's something."

"He's nearly as bad," Ben said. "If we took him to the track, you'd see."

"But we're not going to take him to the track," Dixie said. "Not until he gets over it. Here, let me lead him awhile."

So they kept at the horse, spending all their free time with him and becoming more anxious and determined as the final days of the school term approached. Ben was patient and used all the skill which years of working with Tack Ranch horses had taught him.

"I don't know," he said to Dixie one afternoon dubiously. "He doesn't seem to be like our horses at the ranch."

"Why not?" Dixie replied. "He's got the same kind of brain, hasn't he?"

"He's either smarter, or a lot dumber," Ben said. "I don't know which."

They kept on, working with the horse until dark

every afternoon. In the halter and under the cooling blanket, Peck was a model of deportment, even showing a capacity for affection by presenting his nose to be rubbed. He never showed indication of striking or biting, never even turned aside to prevent being caught. But a bit in his teeth and a saddle on his back started a chain of emotional reaction in his nervous system that seemed to be beyond his control. They petted him and pleaded with him, but still he pranced and trembled.

A Saturday came, the last one before exams.

"Pop'll be coming for us next week," Dixie said.

Ben looked up and nodded. He was busy putting the saddle on Peck.

"Do you think he's about ready?" Dixie asked, meaning the horse.

"I don't know," Ben said.

"If we could show him, we might find somebody that would buy him," Dixie said. "I've got the names of two or three men who are interested in race horses. I could go to the superintendent's office and call some of them."

Ben didn't say anything. He buckled the cinch and tested the saddle for looseness.

"You want me to?" Dixie asked. "We're going to be mighty busy next week."

"I'd better try him first," Ben said. "There's no use having anyone come out if he's going to take the bit in his teeth and run away."

"All right," Dixie said.

They led the horse around the area for some time, to loosen his muscles and get him accustomed to the feel of the saddle. Ben grimaced to himself, thinking how silly this would look on a ranch where time was an important consideration and horses were saddled and mounted with the least possible delay. He wondered if all this pampering which Peck was getting was the best way after all. Maybe having a saddle thrown at him every morning from halfway across the corral would do him good.

Ben mounted and said to Dixie, "I'm going to take him to the track." He rode out of the stable area and, for the first time in weeks, permitted Peck to turn toward the big gate. Immediately the horse's ears went forward and his head came up. He lifted his front feet high and put them down in short prancing strides.

"Take it easy. Take it easy," Ben told him. "This is no race."

But Peck obviously thought it was going to be. He tried to bolt as soon as they were on the track. Ben had to use strength to get him to turn to the left and had to keep pulling him up constantly to prevent him from running. Peck pranced and jigged all the way around the track. When he got back to the gate, where Dixie was waiting, sweat was running down his legs. He wouldn't stand still when Ben halted him, but turned and twisted and backed.

Ben looked at Dixie grimly and said, "What do you think? Still want to have some buyers come out?"

Dixie's pert face with its upturned nose was filled with disappointment. She shook her head and said, "I'll write Pop and tell him to bring the trailer when he comes in after us. I'll tell him we've got a horse to take back."

"Are you going to tell him what kind of a horse?" Ben asked soberly.

"No," Dixie said. "He'll find that out for himself soon enough."

# ◀ • *Six* • ▶

Vince Darby arrived at Aunt Mary's house in the ranch pickup, with the hooded horse trailer behind. He had dressed for the trip in his Sunday clothes, shined boots, wool pants and matching short jacket, and his best soft felt hat. He was a solid man, with iron-gray hair and a tanned, square-jawed face. His eyes were small and penetrating, and he had a habitual squint from days and days in the sun.

"Pop," Dixie cried, "I'm glad you're here. I can hardly wait to get back to the ranch. It feels like years and years."

"It sure does," Vince said heartily. "The place kind of needs you and Ben. Got a lot of riding to do." He winked at her. "Mary, here's a chunk of beef that Milly sent. It's not as fat as I hoped it would be, but it's pretty good. Say, Ben, where's that horse Dixie wrote me about?"

The suddenness of the question somewhat surprised Ben. He gulped and said, "Out at the fairground, Pop. We can go by there on our way out."

"What kind of a horse?" Vince rumbled on. "What're you doing with it?"

Dixie knew Ben would stumble and fumble, so she said blithely, "Oh, we bought him."

"Bought it?" Vince said, the little wrinkles deepening about his eyes. "What for? We've got more horses out at Tack now than we know what to do with. For Pete's sakes, we've got horses to sell."

Ben swallowed again. And Uncle Wes, in his chair, looked a bit gray around the corners of his mouth.

"Oh, we got this one right, Pop," Dixie said. "He needs some work, but we think we're going to make some money on him."

Vince's face relented a bit, and he said, "Going into business, eh? Well, I hope you two don't lose all of your savings. You'd have been smarter to have bought a calf, I expect. How are things with you, Wes? Loanin' lots of money these days?"

"Mmmmmmmm," Uncle Wes said. "Yes, quite a bit, Vince."

"I'll get our things and put them in the pickup, Pop," Ben cried busily. "I'll get them in, and then we can get started." He grabbed an armful of bundles and a suitcase and went out the door.

Good-byes were said and Ben and Dixie and Pop got in the pickup and were off. Pop started out Eighth Street to Overland.

"We've got to go by the fairground," Dixie reminded him.

"Oh yes," Pop said. "I forgot." He made a turn on Front, which led to Fairview.

No one said anything until they got to the fairground. Then Ben said, "Around to the stables, Pop."

"I'll get him," Dixie said, as soon as the truck stopped. She jumped out and went to Peck's stall.

"I'll get the blanket," Ben said, following her. "We don't want to leave that."

"Blanket?" Vince said. "Horse blanket?"

"Yes, sir," Ben said. "The man threw it in."

"Oh," Vince said.

They came out of the stall. Ben had hastily thrown the blanket on Peck and Dixie was leading him. "Come on," Ben said to Dixie. He hurried toward the back of the pickup. Vince hadn't gotten out and Ben hoped he wouldn't.

But Vince's keen eyes didn't miss anything. "Wait a minute," he said, opening the car door. "I'd like to take a look at that horse."

Dixie let Peck come to a standstill. "What do you think about him?" she asked with a cheerful indifference that Ben simply couldn't share. "Looks pretty good, doesn't he?"

"That's a running horse," Vince said, frowning. "You say a man gave him to you?"

"Well, not exactly," Dixie said with an easy laugh. "But to hear him tell it he practically did."

"What's the matter with him?" Vince demanded bluntly.

"The matter—why nothing," Dixie said. "Who said anything was the matter with him?"

"Something is," Vince declared. "Or the man wouldn't have given him to you."

"He didn't," Ben said. "We bought him."

"You couldn't have bought him, not unless there was something wrong with him," Vince said. "I'll bet my hat he's gimpy or something."

"No, he's not," Dixie said. "He's sound as a—a singletree."

"He's a little headstrong," Ben admitted. "He gets excited at times."

"Bolter?" Vince asked, his jaw muscles knotting. "Runs away?"

"Yes, sir," Ben admitted. "But he's a good horse. I'm sure he is, Pop."

"And you think you can break him of it?" Vince said, a certain bitter knowledge in his voice.

"Yes, sir," Ben said.

"Have you any idea how many have tried it before you?" Vince asked.

Ben shook his head.

"Everyone that's owned him, and maybe some others," Vince said. "They've all had a try at it. I know something about these race horse owners myself, Ben. They don't miss anything."

Ben lowered his eyes, then brought them up. "I still say he's a good horse, Pop," he said. "I don't know whether I can train him, but if I can, I know I can make some money on him."

"Not racing him," Vince said flatly. "I'll have no son of mine hanging around race tracks."

"No, sir," Ben agreed hurriedly. "I figure to train him, then sell him to some good owner. I'll have no trouble, once I get him broken in."

"Hump," Vince said. "And you've got it in mind to take him out to Tack?"

"Yes, sir, I'd like to," Ben said, "so I can work him. This is a business proposition, Pop. I'll pay you board on him."

"Board?" Vince said.

"Yes, sir," Ben said, "hay and grain. I know he won't be much good working cattle, but I figure on him to pay his way."

The rancher was silent a few seconds. "It's not that, Ben," he said. "I just don't like to see a son of mine get trimmed on a deal like this."

"I don't aim to be," Ben said seriously.

"He'll sell easy, Pop," Dixie said, "if we can just get him trained."

"We?" Vince said. "How much are you mixed up in it?"

"Half," Dixie said. "He's half mine."

"I might have known it," Vince said. "How old is he?"

"Four," Ben said. "He's not too old."

"But old enough to be spoiled," Vince said. "You know there are no race tracks out at Tack."

"I don't need a track, not for the training I want to do," Ben said.

"No running in the meadows," Vince said. "I can't have all the hay knocked down."

"No, sir," Ben agreed.

"Nor in the brush," Vince said. "He's liable to step in a hole with you. I never saw one of these race horses yet that had any sense about where he put his feet."

"No, sir," Ben said. "I'll be careful. Anyway, what he needs now is slow work. Wouldn't you say so?"

"Hmmmm," Vince said. "How would I know?" Then, as he looked from one to the other of them, his eyes softened. "You two would have to come up with a race horse. All right, let's get him loaded. I hope he's trailer broke."

"Thanks, Pop," Dixie said happily.

"Yeah—sure," Vince said, accepting her hug. "I'm a big sucker."

Ben knew a minute of suspense when the trailer doors were opened, but Peck stepped right in, indicating that he was well accustomed to trailers and vans.

"Good boy," Dixie whispered, giving the horse

a pat on his hard flat hip.

Behind the wheel of the pickup, Vince Darby didn't say much during the long ride down the valley, across the Snake, and out into the rough Owyhee range country. And both Ben and Dixie were mostly silent, knowing that their father, even though he had given in, was not too pleased. Every once in a while, however, one or the other of them would steal a glance through the back window, just to make certain that Peck was coming along all right in the trailer.

They went down the grade into Crystal Creek Canyon in second gear, and Vince made a wide swing to bring the truck and trailer to a halt near the sturdy ranch house. It was late in the afternoon and Steve and Gaucho were in from their work. They came from the house with Milly Darby, in a fresh starched gingham dress, in the lead. She threw her arms about Dixie first and then Ben in a warm hungry welcome.

"I'm sure glad it's summer, Mom." Dixie said. She glanced about at the familiar valley, with its barns and corrals and hayfields.

"I am too," Milly said. "It seems like years since you were here last."

"I second that," Gaucho chimed in, his bright smile

framed by his dark beard. Gaucho had been hired by Vince Darby to break and train colts and from the start, the cowboy had fit right in, like a member of the Darby family, proving his loyalty and industry on many occasions. Strong bonds of affection existed between him and the two younger children. "I could hardly wait for you two to get back," Gaucho went on.

Dixie gave him an impetuous squeeze around the neck. "How's my Listo?" she asked. Though Gaucho's own mare, Listo was Dixie's favorite saddle horse.

"*Bueno,*" Gaucho said. "She'll be happy her Miss Dixie is back."

Steve, who was four years older than Ben and his father's chief mainstay in running the ranch, had little time for sentimentality but plenty for horses. "What's this?" he said, moving around to the trailer. "Where'd you get that old plug?"

"He's not an old plug," Dixie said sharply. "He's our new horse."

"My goodness," Milly said, laughing. "Haven't we got enough horses on this ranch now?"

"Ben and Dixie don't think so," Vince said.

"This is a special one, Mom," Ben said. "I saw him, and I wanted him."

"So we bought him," Dixie said.

"I don't know any better reason for buying a horse," Milly said.

"Maybe we can fatten him up and use him in one of the hay teams," Steve said.

"No such luck," Vince grunted, but with a grin.

"No, sir," Dixie said with determination. "Not this horse. He's hot blooded."

Unperturbed by Steve's joshing, Ben opened the trailer gates and backed the horse out.

"He's a race horse—no?" Gaucho asked, after a glance at the high clean-boned withers.

"You bet he is," Dixie said.

"What do you think of him, Gaucho?" Ben asked, seriously and a bit anxiously, for to him Gaucho's opinion was very important.

"Looks good," the horse breaker said, nodding his head.

"What're you going to do with him, Ben?" Steve wanted to know.

"Ride him," Ben said. "I've got to train him. He needs a lot of work."

"We're going to make some money on him," Dixie said, positively.

"Yeah—how?" Steve asked. Then, disregarding her, he went on to Ben, "Race horses don't have to be trained. All they have to do is run."

"That's what I thought," Ben said. "But there's a whole lot more to it than that."

"Where'd you get him? How much did you pay for him?" Steve asked.

This was a question Ben had been dreading, for he knew the effect a truthful answer would have on his father. Vince, who considered two hundred dollars a fair price for one of his prized Keister colts, would think Ben had lost his mind. But Ben was glad it was Steve who asked, for he could turn Steve's question aside and did. "Oh, I think I got a good buy on him," he said.

"We," Dixie said. "I bought half of him."

"How much, Dix?" Steve persisted.

"Between the two of them," Vince grunted, "I doubt if they could scrape up fifty dollars in all."

"Goodness," Milly said suddenly. "Supper'll be burning. All of you hurry and get ready." She turned and hastened to the house.

"I'll be right with you, Mom," Ben yelled, "just as soon as I put up this horse." He turned toward the barn with Peck at a trot.

"Put Peck in a stall," Dixie called after him.

"Peck?" Steve said. "Is that his name?"

"Part of it," Dixie said. "His real registered name," she went on with that streak of perversity that cropped out at unexpected times, "is Peck o' Trouble."

"What?" Steve yelled, then went into a wave of laughter.

"By George, Dix," her father said, grinning widely, "he is a race horse. With a name like that he has to be."

"Just you wait," Dixie said confidently, "you'll see."

# ◄•  Seven  •►

"Going to ride that new horse of yours today, Ben?" It was after a breakfast of sausage and eggs and hotcakes, and all of them, with the exception of Milly, were headed for the barns and corrals. Ben and Dixie wore their familiar ranch clothes, boots and Levis, light shirts, and felt hats. Pop, Steve, and Gaucho had their specific jobs to do, but Ben and Dixie, in view of their recent return from Boise, had no particular assignments. It was Steve who asked the question.

Ride his new horse? But of course. Ben had been eagerly looking forward to getting Peck away from the race stables, the track and fences, the traffic and paved streets. He held back, however, and said, "I think I will.

I'd like to give him a little work this morning."

"I got your Inky horse up," Vince said. The little black roping horse, named by Dixie in one of her fanciful moods, was a joy to ride and do work on, as well as Ben's favorite of the ranch horses.

"Dixie can ride him," Ben said.

"I'll take Listo, if it's all right with Gaucho," Dixie said.

"*Por cierto,*" Gaucho said. "You will like her, Miss Dixie," he went on, though Dixie had ridden the mare dozens of times and loved her almost as much as Gaucho himself did. Listo, trained and gentled by Gaucho, was truly a horse in a thousand.

"The corrals are full of horses," Vince said, adding pointedly, "good ones."

Ben grinned and said, "There's a good one in the stalls too, Pop."

Gaucho went on around the big barn to the round breaking corral beyond, where he kept and worked his current bunch of colts. Ben, Dixie, Steve, and Vince went to the tack room, got their saddles and bridles, then went to catch their selected horses. Ben found Peck as he had left him the night before, tied securely in one of the barn stalls.

"Good morning, Peck," he said, going in and slipping the bridle on. "You're on a ranch now—a cow ranch, and they don't think much of race horses. There's not a race track in fifty miles. I hope you behave yourself."

He saddled in the stall and pulled the cinch up snug, noticing that Peck's high back carried the stock saddle nicely. He led the horse along the aisle and through the big doorway, and moved him about in a small circle. Vince and Steve and Dixie were coming from the corrals with their horses, Steve already up on Kelly, his leggy gray.

Steve reined up and asked Ben, "Can that horse really travel? I'd like to see him run."

"Don't you worry about that," Dixie said spiritedly.

"How about giving him a spin?" Steve said to Ben, with a daring grin. "I'll match Kelly here against him." Steve was pretty proud of his gray, which was itself half thoroughbred.

Ben shook his head. "Not today. Peck's not ready yet."

"Are you afraid he'll get beat?" Steve asked, still grinning.

"No," Ben said. "He'll outrun Kelly."

"All right," Steve said, "let's see if he can. I'll bet I can beat you to the corner of the upper field." This was a distance of something over a quarter of a mile, which most ranchers considered long enough for a race.

Ben shook his head. He had not mounted yet but was holding Peck's reins. The brown horse had his head up and was showing some signs of nervousness.

"He's a race horse," Dixie told Steve sharply. "Give him time to get acquainted, can't you? You don't handle hot-blooded race horses like you do old cow horses."

"That's right," Ben said, agreeing thankfully.

Vince Darby turned to his own horse and mounted. "It's time we were moving, Steve; we've got work to do," he said. "You two coming with us?" he went on to Ben and Dixie.

"Yes, sir, I am," Dixie said.

Ben wanted to go with them also, but he hesitated, not being quite sure of Peck.

"What're you waiting for?" Steve said to him. "Want me to top him off for you?"

"No," Ben said. "I can ride him."

"Ben has ridden him a lot," Dixie said, from her saddle.

"Okay, let's see it," Steve challenged. "Or let me do it."

This put Ben in a predicament. It had been his intention to warm Peck slowly and mount him in private, not that he was afraid but because that fitted his plans for training the horse. Steve's good-natured taunts, however, caused his indignation to rise. He suddenly turned to Peck, gathered the reins, and stepped into the saddle.

It may have been the strange surroundings or it may have been the other horses, especially the impatience of Steve's mettlesome gray, but something set Peck off. He grabbed the bit in his teeth and bolted. He gave two long neck-stretching lunges, fighting for rein length.

"Yippee!" Steve shouted gleefully and jumped his own horse forward. Having horses buck with him happened so often that he considered this a joke.

"Hold him, Ben!" Vince shouted, concern in his voice. He didn't share Steve's lightheartedness.

But Ben couldn't hold him. Those two desperate lunges had yanked the reins through Ben's fingers and Peck had his head. He knew he was in a race and the fact that the rider on his back was trying to control him meant nothing. Riders always tried to control him, but if he slowed down he got the stick across his tender back. He flashed through the ranch yard, up past the house, and out on the twin-rutted lane that followed the fence around the upper field. He had his nose stretched out and was running with such blind desperation that Ben realized the best thing he could do was try to guide him, to keep him from either hitting the fence or going into the stony ground beside the lane.

"Easy, Peck. Easy," Ben said firmly.

But Peck was beyond reasoning. He was running a race, and through months and months of training it had been drilled into him to win—to win regardless. Later, when he was tiring, would come the bat, as always in the past.

"Yippee!" Steve shouted from behind. "Stay with him, Ben."

Steve was pushing his gray, trying to catch Peck and help Ben, if Ben needed it. And that was just the thing Ben did not want. The pound of hoofs and those of Vince's horse farther back were the things that made it impossible for him to stop Peck. He turned his head and shouted to Steve to pull up, but the wind whipped the words out of his mouth and Steve did not understand. Steve leaned over his gray's neck and urged him to his best speed.

"Pull up! Get back!" Ben shouted.

Back behind Vince, Dixie was coming up fast on the Gaucho's good mare, and she was yelling at them too. Ben knew she was trying to get them halted, but he couldn't watch any longer. He had to turn back to the front, for they were rapidly approaching the corner, where the lane turned at almost a right angle around the fence's big solid corner-post. Peck couldn't make that turn, not at the speed they were traveling. And beyond it, on ahead, there was a stony rising slope, dangerous ground for a bolting race horse.

Ben knew an instant of deep regret of the pride that had caused him to mount the horse, but that was no help now. Now he had either to slow Peck enough to make the abrupt turn or take to the rough ground beyond, an area which he knew well from previous riding. There was a gully out there, not very wide or deep, one which would never cause a good ranch horse an instant's pause, but for Peck, trained on the smooth tracks, it could mean a dangerous fall. Thoughts poured swiftly through Ben's mind. What could he do? Somehow he had to get Peck around that turn—or take his chances with the rocks and gully. If Steve would only pull up, if those hoofs weren't pounding so close behind—

Ben had a sudden thought. Could he do it? With his eye he measured the distance to the corner. It was short, too short—but maybe there was time. He turned for a quick glance behind and saw that Dixie was up with Vince, and Vince, in response to her cries, was slowing down. Steve, however, was still coming, intent on catching Peck and helping Ben.

"Pull up!" Ben shouted, then dared not wait to see whether Steve understood before whirling back to the front.

Then Ben did a strange thing. He loosened the reins, leaned forward above Peck's neck, and shouted in his ears. A new surge of strength flowed through the brown horse and his belly leveled closer to the ground. It seemed to Ben that he had sprouted wings; he fairly flew, his feet seeming not to touch the ground at all. The pound of the gray's hoofs was rapidly left behind. In spite of the circumstances, Ben could not help but thrill to that burst of speed. Still, he could permit it for only an instant. The big corner-post was looming up rapidly. Ben listened to the hoof beats behind, and was pleased that they were much fainter. Then he knew he couldn't wait any longer. He gathered the reins and came back on them with a firm balanced pressure.

"Whoa, Peck. Whoa, boy," he said, keeping his voice even and unexcited. "Whoa, boy. Whoa. Easy, Peck."

The horse's head came up, not much but some.

"Whoa, Peck. Easy, fellow."

Ben put more pressure on the reins. He did not dare saw at them or pull the horse's head to one side, as he might have with a stubborn ranch horse, for such action might cause Peck to fall, and above all things he wanted to keep him on his feet, both for Peck's sake and his own.

"Whoa, boy. Easy."

They were swiftly coming to the corner. Little Inky Inkpot, Ben's trained roping horse, could have stopped dead still in half the distance, but not Peck. Peck had been trained to run, not to stop. He needed room for the springs of his magnificent muscles to run down after the power was turned off.

"Whoa, Peck. Whoa."

The horse's head came up a bit more and Ben felt a shortening of his stride.

"Whoa, Peck. Easy, boy."

Ben put more pressure on the reins, leaned against them. The speed beneath him lessened. Peck's head came up and Ben hoped his eyes were open, hoped he was watching his footing, for now they were at the corner. Now the big post was just beyond Peck's nose. Now was the time.

"Whoa, Peck." Ben hauled back sharply on the reins. This would have set Inky on his haunches, but Peck was trying to stop on his front feet. Now it had to be. Ben laid the right rein heavily against Peck's neck, gripped tightly with his knees and threw his weight to the left, threw it hard and without reservation. Either Peck would come around, or Ben would go off. Ben's shift of weight upset the horse's balance; his inside shoulder dropped low—too low. That was a tense instant for Ben. He hauled back on the reins, to give the horse something to pull against with his head. Peck recovered, and then they were around the corner.

"Good boy, Peck. Good boy," Ben said with deep-felt relief. He loosened the reins enough to steady the horse's stride. Then he became aware that the pounding hoofs were no longer behind him. "Whoa. Whoa, boy," he said, and pulled firmly on the reins.

Peck's head came up. He whistled through his nostrils as he turned his head for a glance behind. There were no pursuing horses back there. The race was over.

Gradually along the grassy lane beside the field fence the big brown horse coasted to a halt.

"Whoa, Peck. Good boy," Ben said and dismounted. And when he was on the ground he found his knees were trembling so badly he could hardly stand.

"Well," said Steve, grinning broadly as he came up. "I'll have to admit he can run. But he got a head start."

Ben felt too weak to argue. Vince and Dixie arrived. They gathered in a little panting group where Ben stood beside the sweat-drenched Peck. Steve was not excited but Vince's face was still a shade grayer than its usual ruddy tan.

"What's the matter with that horse, Ben?" Vince demanded. "Is he loco?"

"No, sir," Ben said. "He just gets excited."

"Well, that's the next thing to being loco, if you ask me," Vince said. "He's dangerous."

"He thought he was running a race," Ben said, "with Steve chasing him. You ought to know better than that, Steve."

"Shucks, I was just trying to help you," Steve said.

"Well," Dixie said, "you made it worse. You didn't have a chance to catch him anyway."

"What I'm concerned about is these crazy streaks,"

Vince said. "Somebody might get hurt."

"No, I won't, Pop," Ben said earnestly. This was what he had been afraid of, and if his father should forbid him to ride the horse all his plans would be ruined. "Honest, he's not mean. He doesn't kick or strike or bite. He's as gentle as he can be. Isn't he, Dix? Dixie and I have been working him for a month in Boise."

"A month?" Vince said. "Well, it doesn't look to me like you've done much."

"Yes, sir, we have," Ben insisted. "He's better now, Pop. Isn't he, Dix? He's getting better. I can bring him out of it; I know I can."

"And what'll you have then?" Vince asked.

"He'll win races," Dixie said positively.

"What good will that do us?" Vince said. "We're not in the race horse business. They're no good for ranch work."

"I guess I'm in the business, in a way, Pop," Ben said. "I own him."

"We own him," Dixie said.

"That's another thing I can't understand; whatever made you buy him?" Vince said. "We've got the best horses in the country, right here on the ranch. What did you want with a race horse?"

"Well," Ben said, "I didn't—not exactly. But I saw him, and he wasn't being handled right. He's a good horse, but he didn't have a chance, not the way he was being handled. Somebody made a mistake with him."

"I'll say they did," Vince said. "I'd just as soon ride a loco burro."

"But I can bring him out of it, Pop," Ben said. "I know I can, if you'll just let me try."

"If you don't get a broken leg first," Vince said. "Is that the reason you bought him, just to see if you could bring him around?"

"No, sir, not exactly," Ben said, struggling with his explanation. "I like him, Pop. I just do. He's a mighty lot of horse. He's big and he's fast and he's honest."

"But," Vince said, "saying he is and saying you can, what'll you do with him? He'll be no earthly good to us here on the ranch. It looks to me like it'll all add up to a waste of time and feed."

"I'll sell him," Ben said seriously. "I figure to get my money back, and more too."

"We will," Dixie said. "We'll sell him."

"How much did he cost you?" Steve asked.

"Enough," Dixie said shortly.

"You're pretty young to start worrying about money, Ben," Vince said thoughtfully.

"I'm not worrying about it," Ben said. "But I thought if I—if we could make some, it would be all right. I know it takes a good bit of money to keep Dixie and me in school at Boise."

"I'll take care of that," Vince said. "I'll keep you in school."

"But what about the note?" Dixie said, her face a mask of perfect innocence.

Ben could have choked her and Vince Darby jumped as if he had been stung by a hornet. "Note?" he asked. "What note?"

"The one Ben and I signed to Uncle Wes, to get the money to buy Peck," Dixie said.

The look on Vince Darby's face was incredulous. "Do you mean, Ben," he said, "do you mean to tell me you borrowed money—borrowed money to buy that—that race horse?"

"Yes, sir," Ben had to say, though the words could barely squeak by the tight place in his throat.

Vince didn't speak for several seconds. "Well," he said. He turned and flicked his horse on the neck with the ends of his bridle reins. "Well—"

"Guess you are in the race horse business," Steve said with a grin. He wouldn't have been disturbed much if the top blew off of old Crystal Mountain.

"I can do it, Pop," Ben said desperately. "I can break this horse and pay Uncle Wes. I know I can, if you'll just give me a chance." He did his best to sound convincing.

Vince held a stirrup and put his foot in it. "It looks like you'll have to," he said slowly. He swung up. "You've made a deal, and it's up to you to keep it. I hope you can do it. But,"—he reined his horse back to add—"watch yourself with that horse. Don't take any fool chances."

## ◄•*Eight*•►

*B*en led the big brown stallion back to the barn. Vince, Steve, and Dixie rode on, headed for the slopes and draws down Crystal Canyon where Tack cattle ranged. Dixie had considered staying with Ben but, when he told her he was going back to the barn, decided to ride on.

Milly Darby came from the house as Ben passed. "Is that the new horse, Ben?" she asked. She had a pan of potato peelings in her hand to throw to the chickens, as if that had been her only reason for coming out.

"Yes, ma'am," Ben said. "What do you think about him?"

"He's good-looking," Milly said. "Did he run away with you?"

"Yes, ma'am," Ben said, grinning. He had hoped she hadn't seen that. "Steve was cutting up," he went on, "and Peck got excited. But he's a good horse, Mom. All he needs is the right kind of handling."

"He seems pretty wild," Milly said.

"Don't you worry, Mom," Ben said seriously. "He's not—really. I can handle him."

"You like him a lot, don't you?"

"Yes, ma'am."

"Why?" Milly asked curiously. "There's some reason, isn't there?"

Ben hesitated and glanced about. This was something he had not intended telling anyone. But he said, "Yes, Mom. Look at his head. It's a lot like King's. When I first saw him I would have sworn he was one of King's colts, he looked so much like him."

Milly knew well how much her two younger children admired the wild black stallion that roamed the Twin Buttes country. "But he can't be," she said. "That's impossible."

Ben nodded. "I know it," he said. "I've got his papers. He's out of a stallion called Big Trouble. I never heard of him before. But he sure does look like old King, Mom, he sure does to me. And if he was—well, you know what a wonderful horse he would be."

"Yes, he would," Milly said.

"I'm going to break him anyway," Ben said. "He's a good horse, I'm sure he is." Ben turned on toward the barn.

"I am too," Milly said.

Ben paused. "Don't tell anyone, Mom."

"I won't," Milly said. She watched them go, the pan of potato peelings in her hand forgotten. "He's a nice horse," she said to herself softly, "and *he's* growing up too."

Ben had told Dixie he was going to the barn, and he did, but when he got there he didn't stop. He went on around the barn to the round corral that lay nearer the creek. This round corral had a high strong fence and was the domain of Gaucho, whom Vince Darby firmly believed to be the best horse trainer in the whole Owyhee range. Ben and Dixie were sure of it, and for years Ben had been going to Gaucho with his major horse problems. In addition to his store of first-hand knowledge, the cowboy could be counted on never to betray a confidence and he was easy to talk to.

A sheepskin-padded Argentine saddle was on a bright sorrel colt and Gaucho was talking to the animal in soft cajoling tones. "*Pobrecito caballo . . . lo siento pesaroso . . . pobrecito*—Hello, Ben," he broke off, looking up. "Why aren't you riding?" To see either Ben or Dixie leading a horse about the ranch was almost unheard of.

"He ran away with me," Ben said frankly.

"Ran away?" Gaucho's dark brows arched questioningly. "But how? You have a bridle?"

"I have a bridle," Ben said. "But I couldn't hold him. He always does that when another horse gets behind him. How can I break him of it, Gaucho?"

Gaucho was no taller than Ben, but his body was strongly knitted and mature. He crossed to the fence with his easy stride and peered through a crack. "He doesn't look bad," he said. "But you're saying he's—difficult?"

"I don't know," Ben said. "I think he's been raced too much. On a race track he goes crazy; you can't hold him or do anything else. He wears himself out before the race starts."

"Ah—race track," Gaucho said, as if that explained something. "Too much for a nervous horse."

"He's not that nervous," Ben said. "He's not really loco, but something happened to him. I don't know what it was. Maybe they started him too young. He's just run crazy. If he thinks there's going to be a race, he gets so excited he just can't wait. The starter ruled him off the track at Boise."

"That's pretty bad," Gaucho said soberly. He stepped up on the fence for a closer look. He climbed over and walked around the brown stallion, eyeing him closely. He paid particular attention to his head and eyes. With a small twig he tapped lightly on the horse's back in the kidney region. "Maybe you went too heavy with the whip," he said, when Peck rolled his eyes.

"I don't use one," Ben said. "I've never whipped him."

Gaucho stepped back and said, "Get on. We'll see."

Ben gathered his reins, measured them, and swung up. Peck started, but Ben halted him with a strong pull and a "Whoa." Gaucho nodded and watched the horse. Peck stood still for only a second or two, then he began to tremble and fret and pull at the reins. He raised his head and watched the colt in the corral.

Gaucho came closer and put his hand on the horse's neck, at the place where it joined the shoulder. He shook his head, wiped the sweat off against his trousers leg, and said, "Get down."

Ben dismounted.

"He's plenty nervous," Gaucho said. "He's confused and he's full of fear."

Ben nodded. "But there must be some way to cure him of it," he said.

"*Sí,*" Gaucho said assuringly. "But it will take work and a lot of time."

"I've got plenty of time," Ben said. "I've got all summer."

"*Bueno,*" Gaucho said. "He has to forget—forget running, forget the race track, forget everything. Then he'll learn. He'll learn the right way this time."

"How'll I do it?" Ben asked. "What'll I do first?"

"Teach him to walk," Gaucho said. "He doesn't know how now. You have to teach him to walk first."

"He won't walk, not under the saddle," Ben said. "He jigs all the time."

"Make him walk," Gaucho said.

"I'll have to lead him," Ben said.

"Lead him. Ride him. Lead him. But all the time—walk," Gaucho said, nodding. "Get on. Get off. Make him too tired to run."

"All right," Ben said.

"Bring me my shoe box," Gaucho said, taking the horse's reins.

"Shoeing kit?" Ben asked. "I'll get it." He hurried to the barn and got the box full of tools Gaucho used to shoe the horses. "What're you going to do?" he asked, when he was back.

"Take off his shoes," Gaucho said, lifting one of the horse's front feet. "If his feet hurt a little bit, he'll have something new to think about when he puts his feet on the ground. It will teach him to be sure-footed."

"Yes," Ben said, feeling that he should have thought about that. He held the reins while Gaucho took off Peck's shoes and used the rasp to take off the thin and broken edges of the hoofs.

"Now he'll learn he has feet," Gaucho said, straightening up with a grin.

Ben nodded. "He probably never had a chance to go barefooted before," he said. "Get your colt. Let's go over across the creek. I want to start working him."

Gaucho shook his head. "Go by yourself," he said. "It's best. Then Peck will pay no notice to anyone else and keep his mind on business."

"Oh," Ben said. "All right. I'll do it. Thanks, Gaucho."

Gaucho's instructions had been simple, but Ben found during the next month that it took an enormous amount of patience to put them into practice. He climbed on and off Peck so frequently that he wore through the leather covering on his left stirrup. His leg got sore from so much lifting and lowering of his weight. Hour after hour, alone behind the trees that bordered the creek, he worked with the horse, talking to him, getting on, and getting off before the nervousness in Peck built up to the breaking point. Off and on. Whoa, Peck. Easy, boy. Walk, walk, walk. Don't get excited. He didn't permit the horse to run a single step that he could prevent. He wouldn't even let him trot. There was nothing but walk and walk, then walk some more. Slow, slow, slow. Take it easy, fellow.

Peck was saddled the first thing in the morning, and he stayed under the saddle at least ten hours each day, even when he was tied in his stall at noon. Ben took the heavy halter and tie rope along on his rides and sometimes would dismount and tie Peck to a tree, leaving him there alone, to fret and twist and turn until he wore himself out.

This monotonous work was galling on the high-spirited brown horse, and he fumed and fretted and neighed and pawed the ground. He would nicker eagerly when he saw Ben returning. Ben paid no attention to the fretting, neither punishing nor scolding.

But progress was slow, discouragingly so. Peck wore out two stout tie ropes, just twisting and turning and tossing his head. And under the saddle he was constantly on the alert for any opportunity to bolt and run.

"I don't know whether I'm getting anywhere or not," Ben said dubiously one morning as he passed the round corral on his way to his favorite training ground across the creek. Peck's fuming and fretting seemed to be worse than usual.

Gaucho paused in his work to look at the horse. "He's better," he said. "I see it in his eyes."

"It doesn't seem so to me," Ben said. "Whoa, Peck. Whoa."

"More work," Gaucho said. "Give him more work."

"But—it's so slow," Ben said.

And Vince Darby thought the progress was mighty slow too. There was hay to be put up and ranch work to be done. Also, Vince had little faith in the whole affair. "The question in my mind," he said to Ben one afternoon, "is, is he worth it? You're sure putting in a lot of time and work on one horse."

"I believe he is, Pop," Ben replied seriously. "I believe he is."

"Well," Vince said, with a shrug of his heavy shoulders, "it's your time and your money—yours," he added with the wrinkle of a grin coming to his eyes, "and Uncle Wes's."

But Milly and Dixie were stanch on Ben's side. "Don't worry about the haying," Milly told Ben privately. "Pop and Steve can handle it." Gaucho never helped, maintaining that he was a horse trainer and didn't know anything about hay. And the horses he trained were so good that for once, though not without an effort, Vince Darby had given in.

Dixie, however, helped with the haying by riding a buck rake behind one of the gentle work teams, and every few days she would search Ben out for a private discussion on the subject of the brown stallion. "How's he coming, Ben?" she would ask. "Is he calming down any? Remember, he's half mine."

Sometimes Ben's answers were optimistic, but often they weren't. Dixie would then reaffirm her faith in the project. "You can do it, Ben," she would say. "He's not a knot-head; he's got plenty of intelligence. You can train him. He'll be the best race horse in Idaho."

So Ben kept on. Even at those times when he was so

discouraged that he thought about giving up, he knew he couldn't—not now. He couldn't give up because of Mom and Dixie and Gaucho and Uncle Wes—they believed in him. And he couldn't give up because of Peck; he knew Peck had the makings of a fine race horse. So he kept on, riding and working the horse, spending hours and hours in the privacy of the flat beyond the creek, riding and dismounting, mounting and riding, tying up and untying. Peck carried Ben's strong stock saddle until he must have thought it was a part of his back, carried it until at last he ceased fretting at it. And he stood tied to a fence or a tree or tied in his stall with a bit in his mouth until he could and often did doze off to sleep. He walked and walked, with Ben in the saddle or Ben leading by the reins. He walked and walked for miles and miles, and was never permitted to run a single step.

One evening Ben came in with a gleam in his eye and could hardly wait to get Dixie aside to tell her. Peck had walked all that afternoon without a single break. He had stopped fretting. He didn't tremble and break out with nervous sweat any more.

"You sure? Are you sure?" Dixie cried joyfully.

"Sure," Ben said. "He's coming along."

"That's progress," Dixie said.

Ben told Gaucho, too.

The horse trainer smiled, his dark eyes dancing merrily. "I knew already," he said. "I saw it when you rode by."

Ben told Milly. He wished Uncle Wes were there so he could tell him too. After that it was much better. He knew he was making progress, knew Peck was, as horsemen often put it, "coming along." Now he could ride without the tiresome dismounting and walking. He could stay in the saddle. And Peck, now that he had learned that he could and had to walk, accepted the gait without complaint. Ben began making long trips, up and down the canyon, being careful of course to stay away from other horses and riders. Peck wasn't ready for company yet, but who said he couldn't walk? He went one day nearly to the top of Crystal Mountain and back, without breaking his stride.

## ◄• *Nine* •►

**B**ut Peck was far from being finished and no one knew it better than Ben. He was walking now, but the time would come when he would have to run again. He would have to be put in company, with other horses. And the big test would come, of course, when he went back to the nerve-racking confusion and excitement of the race tracks. There was a lot of careful and patient work still to be done and no way to be sure of the final results, but Ben was much encouraged. He knew he was making progress. What he had to do now was to keep riding the horse, keep training him in patience and obedience, and be sure that nothing happened that would upset his new emotional balance and spoil him all over again.

One morning he turned Peck's nose up Three Deck trail. The rays of the sun were just breaking over the rim down into Crystal Canyon and he decided he would give the big brown horse a real workout that day. He had another reason too for taking the Three Deck trail; not yet that summer had he been up for a look at the wild bands, at King and his bunch of mares. He knew they were there. Dixie, riding up at the head of Fickle Creek one day with Steve, had seen them from a distance. Ben was eager to see them, to see how the black stallion had recuperated from the severe winter and to see what the crop of colts looked like. He was particularly anxious for a look at Lindy Sue's colt. Lindy Sue was the fine thoroughbred mare that Andy Blair, a racing farm owner from Arizona, had brought to Idaho to run with King's band. King was not a born wild horse but was actually Midnight Chief, the son of old Midnight Fire, a prized racing stallion now dead. He had been stolen from Andy Blair's racing farm when he was just a colt, and in some manner found his way to the wild horses after being abandoned by the thieves. Knowing of King's excellent breeding, Andy Blair was hopeful that Lindy Sue would bear a colt sired by King.

The previous winter had been one of the most severe ever recorded in the West and many wild horses had perished, but Ben and Dixie, with the help of Gaucho and the United States Air Force, had succeeded in saving King and Lindy Sue, along with a few other mares and young colts. Donna Lee, the other mare Andy Blair had brought, disappeared and they never found out what became of her, but could only guess that she had died or been killed by the cougars. Lindy Sue, however, when they had left her in the river breaks, had been in foal and should now have a colt at her side—a wonderful colt it should be, too. Ben wondered if it would be black like King.

Peck's long flat muscles were hardened by much riding and Ben kept him steadily at the twisting, winding path up old Three Deck. Up they went, turn after turn. Peck lowered his head and Ben let him have a loose rein, thinking that a month ago he couldn't have done it. But Peck had come to know that going places over rough trails was a business requiring energy and attention. Also the days when light riders had assailed him with bats and screamed in his sensitive ears were now only dim memories. Sweat presently came to his neck, but it was honest sweat from working muscles, not from the ends of ragged nerves.

Ben flexed his wrist and said, "Whoa," and the big stallion halted and stood still, glad of the opportunity to draw deep refreshing breaths of air into his lungs. He did not move until Ben touched him on. "Good horse," Ben said approvingly. Few things in his life had ever given him the same satisfaction as the knowledge that he was winning this horse.

The warm sun was at its midmorning height when they topped out at the lip of Bascomb Flats. Ben halted Peck and let him blow, looking meanwhile at all the vast Twin Buttes country, at the stretch upon stretch of rolling sage, at the boulder-strewn upthrust of Gailey Ridge, at the dark rising slopes of the Buttes dwarfed in the distance beyond. The sight never failed to thrill him, with its immensity and its secrets, its hidden arroyos, its box canyons, its all-important water holes, its smells of heat and sage and fine dust.

Ben sent Peck on, heading him for old Gailey's broken nose. Up there was a point from which he could view both Bascomb Flats and the wide Juniper Springs country to the south. He had his scarred binoculars along and with any luck at all he should be able to spot some wild bunches.

In the sage, Peck put his head down and walked, walked with willingness and without complaint, answered promptly to signal from hand or heel. Ben forgot his horse and gave his attention to the country, and later on, when he realized this, it amazed and thrilled him. Peck was behaving like any good, well-broken ranch horse. Of course, this was only half the battle, but it was something that had to be accomplished before the rest could be even attempted.

They crossed the miles of dusty sage, and Ben put Peck up the rock-strewn slope. They threaded their way between big sharp-shouldered boulders and came in time to the crest. "Whoa," Ben said and swung down. He didn't leave the horse standing as he would have Inky or Tanger, but looped the reins over his arm while he surveyed the broad stretches of sage with his binoculars. He found dark dots, two bunches in the north in Bascomb Flats and another one in the Juniper Springs area. They were much too far to identify, even with the glasses, and he decided to try the one in Bascomb Flats nearest Basin Lake. He mounted Peck, let the horse pick his way down the north slope, and headed into the sage.

This, however, was not King's band. It was a small

bunch, led by a sorrel stallion. Ben learned this through his binoculars and did not go close enough to disturb the animals. He turned to the right, toward the second bunch, thinking that if this were not King's he would not see them that day, for already it was well after noon and he had been riding steadily since early morning. Peck was learning that legs were for something besides romping around an oval track.

This second bunch, however, was King's. Ben's binoculars told him that while he was still nearly a mile away. He knew the big black stallion too well to need a second look. King's bunch was small too, but that did not surprise Ben, for he himself had seen the heavy kill of the past winter.

The horses were scattered in the sage, feeding. Their condition, Ben noted with pleasure, was good. King was fat and strong again, and his dark coat glistened in the sun. Ben rode closer and swung his glasses around until he found a sorrel mare. That would be Lindy Sue and—yes, there was a little dark colt at her side. This was wonderful. Now Andy Blair had a horse with old Midnight Fire's blood in its veins. Midnight Fire had been killed in an accident, but Andy Blair had never ceased hoping for a colt with his blood lines.

Ben immediately wanted to get closer. Was the foal a filly or a stallion? Andy Blair would be glad to have either, but it made a difference, for a horse colt, if he turned out well, could be used for breeding and could transmit the Midnight strain to many other colts.

Ben spoke to his horse and they moved on through the sage. At a distance of about half a mile, King spotted them. Ben knew it from the way the stallion raised his head. Ben pulled up, becoming a bit dubious. King, of course, would put on his customary show and Ben wasn't certain how Peck would take it. Until now, while riding, he had been careful to keep Peck away from other horses, to avoid any possible excitement.

But he strongly wished to know whether Lindy Sue's foal was horse or filly and, after a few seconds, he rode on. With all that long day's miles behind him, Peck should not be feeling too frisky. Still, he watched the brown horse closely and was aware, by the way Peck's ears swiveled forward, when he saw the wild horses.

"Take it easy, don't be silly," he said. "They're just horses."

Peck went on, still walking, but now his head was up and there was a new interest in his gait. Ben caught the reins a trifle shorter, just to be ready.

The approach became too close for King to endure without action. He arched his neck, tossed his black mane, and sent a trumpeting neigh across the sage. Peck pushed out his nose and answered, and he would have increased his gait if Ben had not held him firmly in control.

Then King came, as Ben had known he would, to make his inspection. He galloped through the sage, head up and neighing, the wind of his movement making dark flags of his mane and tail. Peck halted, surprised and somewhat concerned by the wild stallion's challenging manner. Ben sat still, holding his horse close in precaution, and even in that tense instant he noticed the resemblance between the two. He felt a tremble run through the brown. "Steady, boy, steady," he said. "That's just a bluff. He won't hurt you." And suddenly he lifted his hand, knowing the action would bring King to a halt short of his usual distance.

Earth flew from King's sudden stop. He uttered a loud snort, as much as if to say, "If that man weren't on you, brown horse—" He put a deep, belligerent arch in his neck and began to paw the ground. His neigh had a menacing ring.

"Oh, yeah," Ben said easily. "I know you, you old humbug. Come on, Peck, let's run him off." He touched Peck forward, but was careful to keep him at a walk. The wild horses would be running any minute now.

King snorted and pawed some more, then whirled reluctantly back to his mares and colts. Ben brought his binoculars up and watched the dark colt, knowing that in seconds King would have the whole bunch in flight. If he had been on Inky or Tanger he would have given them a short run, just to see their tails in the air, but on Peck he didn't dare. He couldn't take a chance on Peck, not yet.

The mares snorted and bunched and strung out, and King raged in behind them. Ben let Peck follow, but only at a walk. Then he noticed something: the dark colt didn't run. It merely hobbled along. And then Lindy Sue cut away from the bunch and back toward it. King rushed with bared teeth to turn her, but she evaded him and came on, determined to get back to her colt. King came too, thundering and furious with jealousy.

Ben instantly realized the danger. His hesitation was brief before he clapped his heels to Peck's flanks.

Ready or not, Peck had to run. Ben had known wild stallions to kill colts before when their mothers would not leave them. He did not know that King would, but he dared not take the chance—not with Andy Blair's Midnight colt. One snap of those mighty teeth, and the little animal's skull might be crushed. Ben's heels were rough treatment for a skittish racer, but it couldn't be helped.

Peck was in stride in two jumps. Ben was glad it was only a short distance and over comparatively level ground. He hoped no badger hole lurked there somewhere in the grass. Lindy Sue and King came on, and King was gaining on her rapidly. But Peck was cutting down the distance to the colt with mighty strides. They rushed on, coming together. Ben jerked off his hat and threw it forward. "Get back!" he yelled. "Get back there, you black demon!"

Even in his blazing jealousy, King couldn't stand this. He had been wild ever since he could remember, and men were his enemy, the only creatures that he didn't know how to fight. He halted, glared at Ben, and trumpeted his anger. Ben turned Peck directly at King. King whirled back to his running mares. Lindy Sue slowed to a halt, somewhat suspicious of this new horse and rider, but she would not turn from her colt.

Now Ben had a new problem—to get Peck stopped. He firmed upon the reins and said, "Whoa, Peck. Whoa." Peck tossed his head and fought for the bit. He whinnied after the running wild horses. "Whoa, Peck," Ben insisted. The big horse's stride shortened and gradually he came to a halt. Ben threw himself from the saddle as quickly as he could. Peck was trembling and sweat was popping through the hair on his neck. "Easy, boy," Ben said. "It's all over now. Don't be excited. Nothing's going to hurt you." He rubbed the dark nose gently.

Peck lifted his head, to look for several seconds at the dust of the wild bunch. Then he lowered his head to Ben's hand for more caressing.

# ◄• *Ten* •►

*L*indy Sue was a gentle mare. She had been foaled in a box stall and raised in a small pasture. Men had provided food and shelter for her and had always been her friends. She had no fear of them. She was what is known as a brood mare, dedicated to the business of producing colts—colts made especially valuable by her own fine breeding, her good disposition, and her general excellence of conformation. Had it not been for her colt, she would have run with the wild bunch, but because of habit and not because of fear. However, good mother that she was, her instinct for her colt was greater than her desire for company, even strong enough to make her brave the stallion's anger.

Knowing the mare, Ben approached her quietly

through the brush, leading Peck. "Whoa, Lindy. Whoa, girl," he said reassuringly. She stood near the colt, watching him. "Good girl. Nice Lindy," he said, more anxious now than ever to see the foal.

Lindy Sue may have remembered him from the past winter, when he and Dixie had fed her hard-gained willow twigs from their hands. At any rate, she stood still. The dark colt showed some concern and moved to the mare's far side, but her confidence soon reassured it.

There was keen anxiety in Ben, for he knew the colt was crippled. Otherwise, though still very young, it would have run easily with the mares when they started, and for some distance it could have kept up with them. He hoped it was nothing serious, for this was the colt Andy Blair had gone to such effort to obtain. And this was the only purebred colt there would be, for Donna Lee, the other purebred mare, had disappeared. Colts from the range mares, even though sired by Midnight Chief, could not fill Andy Blair's purpose.

Ben was soon rubbing Lindy Sue's soft muzzle. He looked then at the foal. It was a horse colt, and he knew Andy Blair would be pleased by that. At first there seemed to be nothing wrong with it, but then Ben noticed that its right foreleg, near the ankle, was swollen. He saw the cut. It had not been bad at first, but in some manner it had become infected and now pus oozed from it and the flesh was angry red in color. Ben had seen too many such cuts not to know immediately that it was serious.

"Whoa, little fellow. Easy," he said, moving about the mare so he could see better. He needed medicines, hot water and soap, clean cloths, and disinfectants. And he had nothing—nothing but a pocket handkerchief and that was not too clean.

Ben looked at the wound and calculated the time. By noon tomorrow or shortly after, he could be back, with water that could be heated over a sagebrush fire, and salves, and disinfectants. He could clean the wound and treat it, and return from time to time. But another day would give the infection that much more time to spread. And what if Lindy Sue and the colt moved in the meanwhile? Alone they could be hard to find. What if the colt lay down, as well it might? What if King and the others returned? Or some other wild stallion came?

Ben shook his head. He didn't like it. There were

too many chances, too much uncertainty. He felt that he should have been up here before now, and they should have taken Lindy Sue and her foal to the ranch. But there had been so much to do, and he had been so engrossed with Peck. Now he could take Lindy Sue; he could put his rope on her and she would lead readily, whether Peck liked it or not. But the colt would never make it, not on that injured leg. Even at the slowest pace, the colt would never get beyond Basin Lake.

Ben stood up and looked about, hoping that he might see some help. But few men rode this high wild range. He could, he realized, simply stay where he was, and by noon tomorrow someone from the ranch would be there, looking for him. But he hated the thought of the anxiety this would cause his father and mother, particularly in view of his father's distrust of Peck. And when they came they would have nothing with which to treat the wound.

There was a way, however. If he had been on his Inky horse, Ben would not have hesitated. He looked at Peck and wondered. Would you do it, Peck? And what would such an experience do to a high-strung nervous horse like you? Ben didn't know and he was frankly skeptical. It might send Peck into a frenzy of excitement. He looked again at the dark little colt with its big bright eyes and made his decision. "Okay, little fellow," he said. "This is going to be rough on all of us, but we'll try it. If we don't get you to a doctor pretty quick, it's liable to be too late."

First, he tied Peck by the halter rope to a stout sage. Then he took his lariat from the saddle and made a small loop. He maneuvered around the mare and made a quick toss. The colt went wild as the rope tightened about its neck. He lunged and plunged, heedless of his injured leg. Ben dug his heels into the ground and held. Peck snorted and swung around to the other side of the sage. The colt turned at the end of the rope and laid his full weight against the loop. The loop pulled tighter and tighter about his throat and his big eyes swelled with fear. Ben braced himself grimly, knowing that this had to be. A minute later the colt fell, choked down. Ben ran to his side and, using loops of the lariat, quickly tied his front feet together, then his back feet. He loosened the neck loop. The colt regained its breath and began to struggle to get to its feet. Ben held its head down and talked to it in a soothing voice. "Easy, little fellow. Take it easy. I'm not going to hurt you." After a time the colt lay still, its young flanks heaving.

Ben looked at Peck. "Whoa, boy," he said. "This is where you come in." The brown horse was visibly nervous.

Ben got his arms under the colt's body, gripping the slim legs in his hands to prevent kicking. The colt started struggling again and Ben merely held him until he was quiet. Lindy Sue helped by coming up and nuzzling the little creature. The colt was heavy. Ben could hardly lift it, but he managed to get it up in his arms and walked with it to Peck. The brown's ears came forward and he snorted.

"Whoa, Peck, whoa," Ben said sharply. He stopped and held the colt while Peck's nose slowly came forward for a cautious sniff. "See, it's a horse, just like you," Ben said. "It's nothing to be afraid of." Peck pulled back, dubious and uncertain. Ben waited, holding the little colt firmly to keep it from struggling. Gradually Peck's head came forward, to sniff again. Lindy Sue moved up and stood with her nose at Ben's elbow. Peck stretched his neck over to sniff at her.

"Whoa, Peck," Ben said, and moved in and along Peck's side. Peck sidled away. Ben followed. A clump of sage stopped Peck's sideward movement and he stood, trembling and concerned. "Whoa, Peck," Ben said, and lifted the colt up to the saddle. He balanced the colt with one hand and caught the bridle rein with the other. "Easy, boy."

Ben made a quick hitch about the colt's hind feet. He ducked under Peck's neck, pushed against the sage, and pulled the rope under the horse's belly. It required only a second to make a tie about the colt's front feet, not tight yet snug enough to hold the little animal across the saddle. Ben took a few seconds to soothe Peck, then made a second check of the ropes. The colt would ride there all right, provided of course Peck did not get excited.

Ben untied the halter rope. He let Peck turn his head and smell once more at the little creature on his back. Peck let out a deep breath, and Ben said, "Easy, fellow, easy. Nothing's going to hurt you."

Everything was ready and Ben knew he faced the big test. If Peck was going to do anything, he would do it when he first moved, before he was accustomed to those dangling legs. If he bucked or started lunging, or if he broke away—Ben shook his head. At all cost, for Peck's sake and for the colt's, he had to hold him. He took a firm grip on the halter rope and on the reins together.

"All right, Peck, come on," he said, his voice as casual as he could make it. He turned and started away. Peck pulled him back, too uncertain at first to move. Ben gave him a little time, let him smell the colt's legs again. Then he turned his back and said, "Come on, Peck. Come on, boy."

Peck moved, too rapidly. He jumped. Ben hung doggedly to the rope and reins. "Easy, fellow, easy." Peck swung around in front and came to a high-headed halt. "Come on," Ben said, and started on. Peck followed, jerky and uncertain. Ben kept moving steadily, holding firmly to the rope but not looking back. Gradually the brown horse overcame his nervousness and settled down.

After they had gone a quarter of a mile or so, Ben glanced back to see if Lindy Sue was coming and, as he was certain she would, she was, walking just behind Peck and keeping an anxious eye on her foal. "Come on, Lindy," he said to her. "We're taking your son down to the ranch, where he can be looked after."

Ben knew the distances were long up in Twin Buttes, but he had never before realized just how long. Walking in high-heeled boots surely increased the length of the miles. It was sundown before he reached

Basin Lake. He halted to let Peck drink. Lindy Sue pushed in to gulp the water too, then raised her dripping muzzle to nuzzle the colt. Ben knew the colt was probably thirsty too, and he held some water in his hat to the dark little nose. The colt regarded him with big wondering eyes but showed little interest in the water.

The stars were bright when they reached the top of Three Deck Ridge. Ben went on down the trail without hesitation, thankful he knew it so well. Now Peck followed readily. The steady traveling had eased his concern, and Ben knew he was too tired for more foolishness.

Down the trail they went, around the bends and turns. At places Peck's feet slipped and slid in the loose rocks, and Ben took long steps to stay out of the way. But he didn't halt. "Come on, Peck," he said. He was weary and hungry. He wanted to get to the ranch, to get that colt out of the saddle, and get Peck in his stall. And Peck, for once, was in perfect agreement.

On through the darkness they went, down the slanting trail, around the turns and switchbacks, Ben in front, then Peck with his unusual rider, and Lindy Sue coming patiently and trustfully in the rear. There were no halts to rest—rest could come later. Now the thing was to get down that hill.

They were on the second nose, still high in the darkness above the canyon, when Peck, of his own accord, stopped. The tightened lead reins pulled Ben around and he saw that the horse was staring into the night down the slope. "What's the matter?" Ben asked. He turned back and saw a dark form materialize on the trail, and recognized his father's burly shoulders. And behind Vince there was another rider, one who, from his size, could be none other than Gaucho.

Vince Darby had a flashlight, and the shaft of the light came forward. "Ben?" Vince's voice said. "Ben, is that you?"

"Yes, sir," Ben said. "I'm sorry I'm late, Pop."

The light played over Ben, and over the horses behind him.

"What in the world have you got there—on that race horse?" Vince asked in disbelief.

"Andy Blair's Midnight colt," Ben said.

## ◄ • *Eleven* • ►

"That Peck, he did pretty well, eh?" It was the second day after Ben had come down old Three Deck Ridge in the darkness and the first opportunity he and Gaucho had had to be alone together. A veterinarian had come out from Nampa to give Lindy Sue's colt expert attention. It was, he said, a bad infection, and the colt was weak and he didn't know just what the outcome would be, but he was hopeful. He made an injection of penicillin, left some dressings and salves, and said that time would tell. Lindy Sue and the colt were put in a small corral by themselves, where there would be no disturbances, and Dixie assumed for herself the important job of looking after the little fella. She knew how much Andy Blair had set his heart on having a Midnight colt.

There was a wide grin on Gaucho's face. He was in his round corral and Ben sat on the brown horse outside.

"He sure did," Ben said warmly, leaning forward to rub Peck's neck. "I didn't know whether he could take it or not, Gaucho, but he could. He came down the trail with the colt on his back just like an old mountain horse. Somehow, he seemed to know how necessary it was."

Gaucho bobbed his head in understanding. "Smart horse," he said.

"He sure is," Ben said. "And he's coming along, too."

"It's time he get moving again," Gaucho said.

"But still slow," Ben said, questioningly.

"*Sí,* but not too slow," Gaucho said. "Put him with cows. Cows will be good for him now."

Because of the necessity of getting the hay in the stacks, not much attention had been given to the range where Tack cattle roamed during the past weeks, and Vince was glad enough to turn the job over to Ben. "But remember," he warned, "you're not riding a cow horse. Keep your rope on your saddle and watch out for rocks and badger holes."

Ben promised, and did. He knew better than to try

to rope from Peck's back, but in the days that followed the big horse got a lot of riding. He was under the saddle from morning till night, high on the long slopes of Crystal Mountain or down the canyon to Wolf Creek. One day Ben rode to the base of Bell Mountain, far to the south. Twice he made trips back to Twin Buttes, missing King's bunch the first time but getting a good look at them the second. Ride, ride, ride, mile after long mile. Looking at cattle, rounding cattle, driving cattle. But always at a slow gait, loafing monotonously in the dust, usually alone but occasionally with Dixie or Steve along to lead or haze on the flanks.

The last ounce of fat melted from Peck's big frame. He recognized a job to be done and learned the manner in which to do it. He no longer pranced and fretted; he no longer tossed his head and sweated; he stood still when halted and moved obediently and without fuss when directed. He learned to go around low limbs and pay attention to where he put his feet. Weary muscles at night taught him that energy was something not to be wasted during the day by nervous fretting.

One day, Ben made a test. He was driving a small bunch of cattle through a stretch of good footing near the mouth of Wolf Creek when a steer turned aside. He could have headed it back at a walk and ordinarily would have, but on sudden impulse he jumped Peck to a gallop. Peck wanted to run but Ben held him back and let him overhaul the steer without extending his gait. Then he said, "Whoa," twitched the reins lightly, and was pleased by the horse's immediate obedience. Peck went back to the cattle without fuss or nervousness.

Ben did the same thing again that afternoon, and after that he never hesitated to put Peck in pursuit of a cow when the occasion called for it. At times he even manufactured occasions, just to give the horse an opportunity to gallop. And in this manner, behind slow cattle, Peck learned something that he had never known before, to run under control, to rate his speed in accordance with the demands of his rider.

Ben became confident that he was winning the horse—that he was bringing him to obedience and control. He welcomed the occasions when one of the others rode with him, for it gave him opportunity to handle Peck under familiar conditions and watch his reactions to the presence of other horses. Peck noticed them and would have watched them if Ben had not kept him occupied with his own business. Finally he ceased to pay any attention to them.

One afternoon, when only Dixie was with him, Ben said, "I'm going around the bunch, on a big circle. When I get started, you come after me, but not too fast."

"Want to see what he'll do with another horse behind him, eh?" Dixie said.

Ben nodded and urged Peck to a gallop. The sound of Dixie's horse behind caused Peck to toss his head and roll his eyes for backward glimpses, but Ben held him in close control and soon pulled him down to a walk.

"How'd he do?" Dixie asked, when she caught up.

"Pretty good," Ben said. "He's coming, but he needs a lot more of that kind of work. Another horse coming behind still excites him."

"We'll give it to him," Dixie said.

Four or five days later, Ben made an appointment with Gaucho to meet them at Wolf Creek flats. "I'd like for you to ride him, Gaucho," Ben said, getting down. "I'd like to know if you think he's coming all right."

"*Ciertamente,*" Gaucho said. He gathered Peck's reins and mounted with the sure easy movements of a born horseman. He rode Peck at a trot and at a gallop;

he stretched him out in a short run; he whoaed him and stopped him and backed him up. He rode him while Ben and Dixie galloped about in circles, deliberately, to see if Peck would become excited.

Gaucho had a wide grin on his face when he stepped down. "What do ya think now?" he asked Ben, with a quick assuring nod of his head.

"He did fine, didn't he?" Ben asked.

"*Sí,* he's a good horse."

"It wasn't a fair test," Dixie declared. "Gaucho can handle any horse."

Gaucho handed the reins back to Ben. "You've done a good job, *mi amigo,*" he said.

"Do you think he is ready to go back to the races?" Dixie asked the trainer.

"Oh, no, *señorita,*" Gaucho said quickly. "There must be more work first. He will need to train on a track before it's time for any races."

"A track?" Dixie said. "A race track?"

"*Sí,*" Gaucho replied. "That's where he's scared, no? So that's where he must learn. It will be slow. But he must learn well, or he will spoil all over again. You must be very careful." He turned to his colt and mounted. "You've done a good job, but you're not done yet, Ben," he said before he rode away.

"That's what I think," Ben said, after Gaucho had disappeared along the creek. "He'll have to have work on a track. He'll have to get used to a race track again."

"But how're we going to do it?" Dixie asked. "There are no tracks out here."

"I know it," Ben said. "I wish there were. We could sure use one for a while."

"Maybe we can build one," Dixie said.

"Where? And what with?" Ben asked. "There's not enough level ground, unless we went into one of the fields. You know what Pop would think about that."

Dixie nodded. "It would ruin the hay. Maybe," she went on, with a new idea, "we could send him to Boise. Maybe we could get someone to work him there on the fairground track."

Ben considered that, then shook his head. "Who?" he said. "Anyway, I should be with him when he goes back on a track."

"Why can't someone else do it?" she asked. "There are other good riders, you know."

"Sure, I know it," Ben said. "But they don't know Peck, not like I do. He's a different kind of a horse, and a strange rider could spoil him all over again, if he wasn't careful. I don't want to take a chance on that. He's got to be handled just right."

Dixie was thoughtful for several seconds, then said, "Pop won't let us go to Boise, not now. I wouldn't ask him, even if we had the money. He doesn't think much of this business anyway."

Ben was forced to agree. "No," he said discouragedly. "Gee, Dix, I don't know how we're ever going to get him sold."

"Maybe we can sell him here," Dixie said. "We've sure got to sell him."

"Who to?" Ben said. "Who can we sell him to?"

"Oh, anybody," Dixie said, "anybody who'll buy him. He's a good-looking horse. Someone might come along. Somebody is always coming out here to look at horses."

Ben shook his head. "They wouldn't pay enough," he said. "Anyone who comes out here figures to buy saddle horses. We've got to have more than that for Peck, or we can't get out of debt. We've got to have a lot more than that, if we are going to have enough to pay Uncle Wes and Pop too."

"Gee, Ben," Dixie said, "how much do we owe?"

"I don't know exactly," Ben said. "But it's plenty. Peck's been eating a lot of hay and grain."

Dixie didn't reply for several seconds, then she said, "Sometimes it kind of scares me, Ben."

"Scares you? Why?" Ben asked.

"I don't know. We owe so much. What if we couldn't pay it?"

"We'll pay it," Ben said stoutly. "We've got Peck. We'll pay it when we sell him, even if we can't get all that he's worth."

"But what scares me is something might happen," Dixie said.

"What're you talking about, Dix?" Ben said. "What could happen?"

"Oh, sometimes I get to thinking," Dixie said. "Suppose he got sick or something? Suppose he broke a leg?"

"Gee whiz, what's the matter with you?" Ben asked irritatedly. "Why should he get sick, or anything like that?"

"I don't know," Dixie said. "But it happens, you know that. Remember Steve's Cougar horse."

Ben did, very clearly. Cougar had broken his leg in a fall three years before and it had been necessary to put him out of his misery.

"But, Dix—" Ben said.

"You'd have to sell Inky," Dixie said. "That would be the only thing left to do."

"I won't," Ben said sharply. Then he added, "I mean

I won't—not unless I have to."

"You promised Uncle Wes," she reminded.

"I know I did," Ben said with exasperation. "Gee whiz, Dix, why do you have to bring that up? Don't you think I've got trouble enough already?"

"I think we'd better get some insurance," Dixie said.

"Insurance? What for? Insurance costs money," Ben said.

"Just the same, we'd better get some," Dixie said. "Pop is going to town tomorrow. I'll go in with him and have it fixed up."

"What fixed up?" Ben said. "What've we got to insure?"

"Peck," Dixie said, "so if he gets hurt or gets sick and dies. We'd at least have enough money to pay Uncle Wes."

"Where'll you get the money?" Ben said. "It took all we had to buy feed in Boise."

"I'll borrow it," Dixie said.

"Who from?" Ben asked.

"Uncle Wes," Dixie said.

"Do you think he'll let you have it?" Ben asked.

"He will when I tell him what it's for," Dixie said. "He's that smart."

"Oh, all right," Ben said, "but it seems like we just

have to spend more and more money. We're getting deeper in debt all the time. Come on, it's time we were getting back or we'll be late for supper. Darn it!"

They rode back along the Crystal Creek trail in silence, both of them lost in their own unhappy thoughts. They forded the creek, went up past the round corral, and on to the barn, and there Ben learned what had brought the dismal subject of sickness to Dixie's mind.

In front of the tack room Vince Darby was leaning both arms on the top rail of the corral fence, staring moodily across the canyon. He roused himself when he heard them and turned briefly to see who it was. He turned back without speaking.

"Hi, Pop," Dixie said, her voice low and dispirited.

"Hello," Vince replied gruffly.

"What's the matter? What is it, Pop?"

Vince was slow in answering, but Dixie knew. She said, "The little Midnight colt is dead."

Ben remembered then that it was Dixie who had been doing most of the looking after the little animal. "No," he said, hoping desperately that it wasn't true.

Vince Darby nodded his big head.

## ◄• *Twelve* •►

*T*he next day, when he and Dixie were in Boise, Vince Darby sent a telegram to Andy Blair, but Andy had already left his home in Arizona. He was en route to Idaho, in response to the letter Vince had written him. And, as luck would have it, he arrived at Tack, pulling a trailer behind his heavy sedan, just two days after the Midnight colt's death.

Vince and Steve were in the hayfields and Gaucho was working a colt somewhere beyond the creek. Ben and Dixie were riding up on Crystal Mountain when the car came over the shoulder and started down the long grade. "That's Andy Blair," Ben said, guessing correctly.

"Oh, no," Dixie said. "Didn't he get Pop's telegram?"

"I don't know," Ben said. "Likely not. Anyway, I think that's him."

"Come on," Dixie said, and turned her horse down the slope. "I guess we'll have to tell him."

"I sure hate to," Ben said. "He's sure had hard luck, losing Donna Lee and now this colt."

Andy Blair pulled his car into the yard and stopped. He saw Ben and Dixie coming down the slope and waved to them. He sat in the front seat, his long booted legs out the open door, and waited for them. "Hi, Ben. Hi, Dixie," he greeted as they rode up and he stood up to shake hands. He was a big spare man and moved with the weariness that comes from long driving.

"Hello, Mr. Blair," Dixie said. "It's good to see you again."

"It's good to be here," Andy said heartily. "Where's your father?"

"Down in the lower field," Ben said. "He's stacking hay."

"Stacking hay, eh?" Andy said. "I wish I had a good hay meadow on my place. Vince wrote me that you've got a colt for me—a Midnight colt." The look on his face was pleased and happy.

Ben looked down at his saddle horn, leaving Dixie

to reply. There was a long depressing silence, broken finally by the Arizona man himself. "What is it?" he asked.

"We did our best, Mr. Blair," Dixie said. "Ben brought him down from Twin Buttes across his saddle, and we had the doctor out from Nampa—"

"He's dead," Andy Blair said, his face becoming suddenly weary. "He didn't make it."

"No, sir," Ben said. "He—he didn't make it."

"I'm so sorry, Mr. Blair," Dixie said. "He was a great little colt, too. We don't even know how he got hurt."

"It was all festered and infected when I found him," Ben said.

Andy Blair took a few steps backward and sat down again in the car seat.

"I'm sorry you made the long trip up here," Dixie said.

"That doesn't matter," he said. "That's the horse business for you," he went on presently. "You work and try, and plan and build, and then you lose them. There are a lot of disappointments—but there are some fine successes too. I wouldn't do anything else."

"Yes, sir," Ben said, happy to agree if it made Mr. Blair feel better.

Milly Darby came from the house. "Andy Blair," she cried, "I didn't know you were here."

Andy stood up and shook her hand. "I sure am, Mrs. Darby," he said. "I just got here. Ben and Dixie were coming down the hill."

"Did they—" Milly asked, regretfully.

"Yes, they told me," Andy said. "I guess its not meant for me to have a Midnight colt. I'm sorry, of course. But it can't be helped, so let's not worry about it. How's Vince?"

"Fine," Milly said. "Ben, go tell Vince that Andy is here. It's about time for them to quit anyway. Come on in the house, Andy. You'll stay a few days with us, won't you?"

Andy Blair nodded. "A day or two, if you'll let me," he said. "Say, Dixie, where is Lindy Sue? I'd like to see the old girl and tell her hello."

"In the little corral," Dixie said. "Come on. I'll take you down there."

Riding to the field, Ben couldn't help but feel sorry for Andy Blair. It was a shame to lose that colt, after all the trouble Andy had gone to. And to lose Donna Lee, too. There was only Lindy Sue left to go back to Arizona. Then an idea came to Ben, an idea so exciting that he tried to put it out of his mind. But it kept coming back. It was a chance, the perfect answer, if he could just work it. The more he thought about it the more certain he became. He knew, however, that it wouldn't just happen, not by itself, it would have to have some help. And all through supper that night he could hardly eat, from wondering how he could give it the help it needed.

When Vince and Andy Blair went into the living room to sit and talk awhile before bedtime, Ben went right with them. Gaucho and Steve got out the checkerboard for a game, but Ben stayed with his father and their visitor. And as soon as the dishes were done and the kitchen tidied up, Milly and Dixie came in.

The conversation stayed away from colts, but it couldn't stay away from horses, not with so many recollections in the minds of these two men, and occasionally, in talking about horses he had raised and others he had known, Andy Blair mentioned the activity on his breeding farm in Arizona.

"Do you train race horses at your place, Mr. Blair?" Ben asked when he found opportunity to squeeze into the talk.

"Some," Andy Blair said. "But mostly we concentrate on raising and selling yearlings and two-year-olds to men who follow the races."

"Do you have a track?" Ben asked.

"Yes," Andy said. "It's not exactly a track, but it looks like one, with an outside fence and a rail. We breeze the youngsters on it when we're getting them ready for a sale. I believe they bring better prices if they've been legged up a bit."

"Do you have a trainer?" Ben asked.

"I've got a man," Andy said, nodding.

"Is he a good trainer?" Ben asked. "Does he really know how to handle race horses?"

"Well," Andy Blair said, a bit puzzled, "I think he is. He's had a lot of experience. Why are you so interested, Ben? Are you by any chance looking for a job?"

Before Ben could answer, Vince said, somewhat drily, "Ben's a race horse owner now, Andy. He bought a race horse last spring."

"And me," Dixie said.

"Yes," Vince said. "Dixie's got a half interest in him."

"Well," Andy said to Ben, "that's interesting. Is he a good one?"

"I think so," Ben said.

"Has he won any races for you?"

Ben shook his head. "We haven't raced him, not yet."

"Why? Is he too young?" Andy asked.

"No, sir," Ben said. "He—he was a little spoiled."

"Runs away," Vince explained bluntly. "He takes the bit in his teeth and you can't do anything with him."

"Oh," Andy said, with a touch of regret.

"Not now, he doesn't," Ben said. "I've been working him all summer. I've got him about cured."

"Sometimes that's pretty difficult to cure," Andy said.

"I know it," Ben said soberly. "But I think he's all right now."

"Is he a thoroughbred?" Andy asked.

"Yes, sir," Dixie said proudly, "one hundred per cent pure."

"Do you know anything about his breeding? What's his sire?" Andy asked.

"Big Trouble," Ben said. Andy didn't reply, and Ben asked, "Do you know anything about him?"

Andy shook his head. "I don't know him. But," he went on kindly, "that doesn't necessarily mean anything. There are probably a lot of good stallions I never heard of."

"His dam was Miss Peck," Dixie said.

"I've heard of her," Andy Blair said. "She's a good

mare, well-bred and with quite a track record. Who owns her now?"

"We don't know," Ben said.

"Where was this horse of yours raised?" Andy asked.

"We don't know that either," Dixie said. "We bought him in Boise. We went out to the races one afternoon and saw him."

"Did he win?" Andy asked.

"No, sir," Ben said, hoping it would go no further than that.

But Andy said, "Where did he finish?"

"He didn't," Dixie said. "They ruled him off the track, because he wouldn't start."

"Oh," Andy said. "That's too bad."

"But he would have won, if they had let him run," Dixie said stoutly.

"I think," Milly said, "that is the reason they bought him, because they felt that he didn't have a fair chance. He is really a very nice horse."

"I'll admit he has surprised me," Vince said. "Ben has been getting a lot of work out of him lately—for a race horse."

"Oh, it's not unusual for a thoroughbred to make

a good stock horse," Andy Blair said.

"I know that," Vince said, "but most of them that do have never been used for racing. Racing spoils them for nearly everything else. And at the price, they come pretty high for saddle horses. Give me Morgans or Arabs or quarterhorses, with a little dash of sagebrush and rimrock stock thrown in to make them tough. That's what a man needs when working cattle."

Andy Blair smiled, for this was an argument that went on heatedly wherever horsemen gathered. "What are you going to do with this horse of yours, Ben?" he asked.

"We're going to sell him," Ben said.

"We've got to," Dixie said. "We're in debt for him," she went on to explain with that characteristic frankness which Ben often found embarrassing.

"Well," Andy Blair said, "that does present something of a necessity, Dixie. I've experienced it at times in my own business. Do you have any prospects?"

"No, sir," Dixie said.

"The trouble is," Ben said earnestly, "we never have a chance to show him. Buyers looking for race horses never come out to a ranch like this."

"No, I guess that's right," Andy said. "You should

take him to a sale someplace."

"That's what I want to do," Ben said. "That's what I'll have to do. That's what I wanted to ask you, Mr. Blair. He needs a little more training on a track, and then he should bring a good price. Do you know a place where I could take him?"

"Why," Andy Blair said, thinking hard, "why, sure I do, Ben. My place. There's a track to work him on, and they hold sales around there and over in California all the time."

"That would be fine," Ben said, not daring to look at his father. "I'll pay you for it, Mr. Blair. I can't go unless you'll let me pay you, for board and horse feed and everything—when I sell Peck. Will that be all right?"

"But, Ben," Vince said, "you can't do that. How do you know you'll get enough for Peck to pay everything, with what you already owe Uncle Wes? You're getting into this way over your head."

"That's the only chance I have, Pop," Ben said. "I'll never get enough for him here."

"That's right," Milly said. "He's got to take the horse where there are buyers."

"I'll pay you. I'll pay you when I sell my horse. Is

that all right, Mr. Blair?" Ben asked.

"Sure," Andy Blair said. "That's all right, Ben. I'll wait for my money until you get your horse sold. And you can go down with me when I go back. There'll be plenty of room for your horse in the trailer, too."

Dixie spoke up then. "Me, too, Ben," she said with determination. "We'll have to pay my board too. Don't forget, Peck is half mine."

"But, Dixie—" her father said.

"Why not?" Milly asked. "If Andy will have room for her."

"Sure I will," the big man said. "Sure I'll have plenty of room for them both."

"Her name is on that note to Uncle Wes as well as Ben's," Milly said, looking at her husband. "There's no reason why she shouldn't go."

"All right," Ben said, "she can go, Mom. I'll take her. I might have known that I couldn't get away without her anyhow."

"When do we start?" Dixie asked.

"Whew," Vince Darby said, shaking his head as if somewhat dazed. "If you ask me, you three are sure putting a big load on one race horse."

## ◄• *Thirteen* •►

*T*hey reached the Andrew Blair place just at dark. During the day they had driven through mountains and timbered country, across deep canyons, and through high dry stretches of desert and greasewood, but Andy's ranch, when finally they reached it, was in the midst of a flat farming community, not far from a good-sized city. It lay right next to a big hard-surfaced highway and all around there were white plank fences and other houses and barns. And Andy's whole place, including the ground the house and buildings stood on, and the small orchard, was not as big as the biggest of the hayfields back at Tack.

Ben was disappointed. He didn't say so, of course, but it didn't seem to him that there was room on the place really to ride a horse. All the fences were much too close and too white.

Andy Blair halted the car in an area between two white rows of stables and sounded the horn. By the time they were out of the car, a man had appeared. "Hello, Fred," Andy said. "I'm back. This is Ben and Dixie Darby. There are a couple of horses in the trailer. Will you look after them?"

"Yes, sir," the man said. "How is the Midnight colt?"

"We lost it," Andy said. "I brought the mare home, and one of Ben's horses. How is everything going here?"

"Fine," the man said. He went to the back of the trailer and opened the doors. "It's too bad about the colt."

"Couldn't be helped," Andy said. A woman came across the area just then, and Andy greeted her warmly. "Mom," he said, "this is Ben and Dixie Darby. They have come down to stay with us awhile and train a horse."

Mrs. Blair was a nice-looking gray-haired woman. "Oh," she said, "you are those two marvelous children from the Darby ranch. Andrew has told me all about you, and the way you ride and handle horses.

Sometimes I find him hard to believe."

"Yes ma'am," Ben said, feeling his face turn red.

Dixie bobbed her head in a kind of uncertain way, as if not quite sure whether Mrs. Blair was serious.

"You won't," Andy told his wife, "not after you've seen them. Horses are second nature to them."

"We'll pay for our room and board, Mrs. Blair," Dixie said.

"It's strictly a business venture," Andy explained. "Ben and Dixie bought a race horse that they expect to make some money on."

"We have to go to Boise to school," Ben said. "And that takes extra money."

"I see," Mrs. Blair said. "Well, we're glad you picked our place for your training. Maybe we had better go to the house. I expect you're hungry."

"Yes, ma'am," Dixie said.

"Could I look after my horse first, please?" Ben asked.

"Of course," Mrs. Blair said. "Come to the house when you've finished."

The house was as surprising to Ben as Mr. Blair's "ranch" had been. It was a low rambling building of brick and tile, half covered by vines. Inside there were thick rugs on the floors, numerous pictures on the walls, and big soft chairs and sofas. There were floor lamps and table lamps with big spreading shades, and heavy curtains at the windows. Everything was so nice that Ben felt somewhat out of place, but Andy Blair took him along a hall to a room and said, "This is where you'll bunk, Ben. Just make yourself at home. This is kind of a lazy household, everyone does just about what he wants to — even the hired people. Dixie's room is just across the hall. Come to the living room when you're ready."

"Yes, sir," Ben said. And after Mr. Blair was gone, he stood looking about, not knowing just what to do first.

The door opened softly and Dixie slipped into the room. "Jeez, Ben," she whispered, for once in her life really impressed. "Mr. Blair must get a lot for his colts."

"He must," Ben said. "This is sure nice. But where do we wash?"

"In the bathroom, of course," Dixie said.

"But where is it?" Ben said.

"Well," Dixie said, "it should be either that door or this one." She opened a door and revealed a bathroom done in salmon-colored tile. "The other one is the clothes closet," she said.

"Boy!" Ben said, looking in. "You first, Dix."

She shook her head. "There's one in my room too, only it's white," she said. "Be sure you don't leave any rings around the tub."

It was daylight but still very early when Ben awoke the next morning. He listened. Everything was quiet in the house. Ben got up, unable to wait any longer. He dressed in his boots and clean shirt and Levis quietly, so as not to awaken anyone else, then tiptoed down the hall to the living room.

"Pssst."

Ben turned. There was Dixie, also dressed in riding clothes. "Where're you going?" she whispered.

"Out. To look at the stables," Ben whispered back.

Dixie nodded and said, "I'll go too."

Just then a door opened and Andy Blair said, "What're you two whispering about? Come on in the kitchen; breakfast is ready." He grinned good-humoredly.

From the breakfast nook windows, while they ate sausages and eggs and hotcakes with tasty syrup, they could see to the rear of the house where, on a somewhat lower level, there were the stables and barns and corrals which were the heart of Andy Blair's breeding farm.

Ben was at once struck by the well-kept appearance of everything. The fences and stables were freshly painted, and the stables had front overhangs and their roofs were green. At one side there was a small white house, with vines growing up its side and on across the roof.

Horses were in several of the small corrals near the stables, and beyond the stables, on the far side of a long white fence, a number of horses could be seen in what was obviously a pasture. Horses' heads were visible in several of the stall doors in the far row. All the fence gates were closed and the whole place had a picked-up look, without any rubbish or gear lying about.

"You've sure got a lot of nice stalls," Dixie said to Andy Blair.

"I don't see the race track," Ben said.

"It's back in the pasture," Andy said. "You see a part of the fence, over there to the left."

Ben saw it then, a long oval, partly hidden by the farther stables. "That's fine," he said. "That's just right."

"There's a starting gate there too," Andy said. "I like to get the colts used to it early."

As soon as breakfast was over, they went to the stables. Fred Ward, the foreman, and two more men were feeding and watering horses and cleaning stalls. One of the men was small, not as large as Ben but several years older, and Ben knew at once that he was or had been a jockey.

"How're the horses this morning, Fred?" Andy asked.

"Good," Fred answered. "The colts are doing fine."

"There's Peck," Dixie said, noticing a horse in one of the stalls.

"I'll get him," Ben said.

"Fred," Andy said, "Ben has brought a horse for some training. He gets pretty excited in a race. I told him we would help him in any way we can."

"Yes, sir," Fred said, looking at Peck. "He's a big leggy animal. We could let Troy give him a workout. Troy is a good rider."

The smaller of the two other men heard this and came toward them. Ben knew this was Troy.

"Troy has ridden in a lot of races," Andy told Ben.

The little man nodded his head and said confidently, "I can bring him around. I know his kind."

Ben shook his head. Troy was too cocky, too sure of himself. "I want to ride him first myself," Ben told Andy Blair, "till he gets used to the track and everything."

Andy nodded and said, "You handle him just like you want to, Ben, and tell us if you want any help. Use the track all you wish. Fred, we'll need a horse for Dixie to ride."

"What kind?" the man asked, looking at Dixie.

"A good one," Andy said. "And don't worry whether she can handle him."

"How about Duke?" Fred asked. "He's a good horse."

"Not good enough," Andy said.

Mrs. Blair had come from the house and was listening. "I know," she said. "Let her ride Sunday."

"Sunday? but that's your personal horse, Mrs. Blair," Fred said.

"Sure," Andy Blair said. "You'll like Sunday, Dixie. He's just your kind. As a matter of fact, he's a Keister colt from Tack Ranch and Gaucho broke him."

"I remember him," Ben said. "He's that dark bay you bought from Pop, the first time you were up there. He would be just right for you, Dix."

"And you're welcome to him," Mrs. Blair said. "He doesn't get enough riding anyway. He's beautifully mannered and I'm sure you will feel right at home on him."

Dixie had been strangely silent during all this conversation, and now she cocked her head to one side and said, "I thought this was a running horse outfit, Mr. Blair. Haven't you got some good young colts that are broke to ride but need exercising?"

Andy Blair's eyes widened, then he said, "I sure have, Dixie. I have a lot of them. But that's work. I hire people to ride them."

"How about hiring me?" Dixie said. "If you find I can't do the job, you can fire me. What do you say?" When in this mood, Dixie had a way about her.

Andy Blair regarded her speculatively for several seconds, then he said, "How much? I always like to know what I'm paying a hand."

"If you want to pay me, I'll work reasonably," Dixie said. "What do you say to my board and room, for a time till we see how I come along? What do you say to that?"

"It's a deal," Andy Blair said heartily. "Troy," he went on, turning to the jockey, "here's your new assistant. Fix her up with a good light saddle and see that she gets plenty of colts to work. And you stay with her. Something tells me we're going to get some real work done on this place for a while."

The little rider grinned and nodded his head. "Yes, sir," he said. "I'll look out for her. Yes, sir. I'll see that she gets plenty of riding."

"Good," Andy Blair said.

"All right, let's get started," Dixie said.

# ◄• *Fourteen* •►

*B*en found his bridle and saddle in the tack room at the end of the east row of stables. Peck, around those stalls so much like race horse barns, seemed a bit nervous this morning. He kept raising his head and looking around.

"Whoa, Peck," Ben said, and put the bit in the horse's mouth. He put up his saddle, settled it, and drew the cinch up snug. Peck twisted around and lifted his head to watch Troy and Dixie, who were readying horses from the west stalls.

Peck *was* nervous this morning. Possibly the long ride in the trailer with Lindy Sue had something to do with it. Ben could sense the tension in the horse, and it worried him. Peck was showing signs of his old track fever.

"Ready, Ben?" Dixie called. She and Troy had finished putting saddles on two trim colts. Fred was waiting to go with them to the field gate and help them mount.

Ben shook his head. "You go ahead," he said. "I'll come on later."

"Okay," Dixie said. They took the colts to the field gate, went through and mounted, Dixie getting up on a beautiful sorrel. They rode on, down the gentle slope toward the track, holding the young racers in tight control.

Ben knew a minute of concern about Dixie, for despite her confidence and ability she was accustomed to the security of a stock saddle and to well-trained and dependable horses. She looked awkward in those short stirrups. But so, for that matter, did Troy.

Ben didn't mount but led Peck about, here and there and in aimless circles. The horse, however, didn't calm down. Sweat soon appeared on his neck and shoulders. Ben kept leading. He took the horse out of the stable area and to the corrals behind. In the largest, a round longeing corral built especially for training and with a good strong fence, he led Peck around and around. But nothing this morning would calm the horse. He rolled his eyes at the white fences and kept his ears cocked to the whine of traffic on the big through highway beyond Mr. Blair's house. Ben felt some sympathy for the horse. All this was greatly different from the long slopes and quiet meadows at Tack; it even distracted and annoyed Ben.

Troy and Dixie came back. They dismounted at the gate and led their sweated horses through and on to the stalls. The horses' nostrils were big and open, showing their recent exertion, and they lowered their heads and snorted to rid their noses and throats of dust. This sound caused Peck's head to come up and he began to fret and fume.

"Gee, Ben," Dixie said, her eyes shining. "I hate to take the money. This Dolly is a sweet filly. She can fly."

"What happened to you?" Troy asked. "We thought you were coming out to the track."

Ben shook his head. "My horse isn't ready," he said.

"Not ready?" Troy said. "What do you mean?"

"He's a little stiff," Ben said. "I don't think he's over the trip yet."

"He's not hurt?" Dixie asked quickly.

"No, he's all right," Ben said. "He's just a little upset, that's all."

"Oh," Troy said, and there was a questioning in the

word that Ben did not entirely like.

Ben put Peck in his stall and returned to watch the colts.

"You want to lead these horses and cool them?" Troy said to him presently. "We'll have time to breeze a couple more before lunch, if you will."

Ben couldn't very decently say no. He took the lead ropes and led the two horses slowly about in the area between the stables. This cooling after exercise was an old story to them and they followed willingly.

"You can give them a little water, but not too much," Troy said. "Then lead them till they're dry." He turned with Dixie to the stalls for two more colts.

Ben didn't say anything. He took the horses by the watering trough and let them have a few gulps, pulling them away, however, before they could get enough to make them sick. Didn't Troy Lane think he knew how to take care of horses? He led them for another three-quarters of an hour, until their coats were dry and he was certain they were cool, then let them have all the water they wanted. He took them back to their stalls, found a curry comb and brush, and gave them a brisk grooming. And he could not help but notice their splendid condition as indicated by their shining coats.

Troy and Dixie came back, again leading sweated horses. Dixie's eyes were bright with the excitement of fast riding, and her cheeks were rosy under their freckles. "They're great, Ben," she said, meaning the horses. "You just sit up there and hold them steady. They've got the longest, smoothest strides. Mr. Blair has sure got some fine colts."

"Uh-huh," Ben said, nodding. They were beautiful colts, trim, sleek, and racy; but, he went on to himself, no better than Peck. If Peck had had the same chance, the same careful training and conditioning, he would have been just as good as any of them.

Andy Blair came from the house. "Lunch time," he called, and waited for them to accompany him back. "How did it go, Dixie?"

"Good," Dixie said. "You've got some nice colts."

"Have any trouble with them?" Andy asked.

Dixie shook her head. "I got along all right. Troy Lane is a good rider. He knows just how to handle them. You just have to watch them closer than you do saddle horses, that's all."

"I'm glad you like them," Andy said. "I believe they're the finest bunch I have ever raised. We'll have them in tiptop shape for the sales this fall."

"I rode one called Dolly," Dixie said. "She's a honey."

"She is exceptional," Andy Blair said. "She may be even better than I think she is. I might put her in a race or two before I sell her, just to see how she goes."

Ben felt rather out of it. Andy Blair did not ask him about Peck. But of course, with Dixie talking so fast, Andy didn't have much of a chance. And if he had asked, there wasn't much Ben could have said in reply—not much that was very cheerful anyway.

The next morning Ben rode Peck, but alone and after Troy Lane and Dixie had gone to the track. He did not go to the track, but stayed around the stables and in the big training corral. Peck still showed signs of nervousness, and that worried Ben. Of course, it might be just the long trip and the strange place, but Ben wished Gaucho were there, so he could talk to him about it. He could have talked to Andy Blair, but he felt that Andy didn't know horses, not like Gaucho did. And he didn't know Fred Ward and the other men well enough to take them into his confidence—certainly not Troy Lane.

Troy was nice enough, and he was kind to Dixie, helping her saddle and telling her how to ride and handle the young running horses. He was in turn amazed by her understanding of horses and her natural riding ability, and he did not hesitate to speak frequently in her praise. "She's a great little rider," he told Andy Blair within Ben's hearing. "She's smart with horses, but still she has plenty of spunk."

Ben felt his face start to turn red and he ducked out of sight into Peck's stall. Did Troy think Ben lacked courage? Was that the reason he emphasized Dixie's bold riding? The very idea caused Ben something of a shock, but, reflecting back on Troy's attitude toward him and other remarks the jockey had made, he realized that it was likely true. Evidently Troy did not think much of his riding ability or his riding courage. Ben couldn't help but feel irritated.

And one morning a few days later when, as Ben was saddling Peck, Troy Lane said in a low but superior voice, "Want me to ride that horse for you? I'll put him in the groove," Ben couldn't keep back a quick flush of anger.

"When I want your help, I'll let you know," he said shortly.

"Oh, all right," Troy said. "It just looks to me like you're having a lot of trouble with him. If you ask me, you're coddling him too much."

"I haven't asked you," Ben said, unable to keep his jaw from tightening belligerently.

"No, that's right, you haven't," Troy said, in a tone which indicated that Ben would have been smarter if he had asked.

Ben bit his lip and turned away, knowing that it would certainly be unseemly to come to an open quarrel with one of Andy Blair's hired men. Too, it would make it unpleasant for Dixie, since she rode almost daily with the jockey. But Ben was irritated and incensed. He was certain in his mind that Troy did not know as much about horses as he thought he did, and he would have enjoyed telling him. In fact, the thought was so maliciously pleasant that Ben hoped the opportunity would come for him to do it, though of course in a manner that would not be troublesome for Andy Blair.

That morning, after he had mounted Peck, he had an impulse to ride to the track, just to show Troy he could handle him. Maybe Peck *was* all right. Maybe it was true that he was coddling him too much. Maybe Troy was right and it was Ben who was wrong. For a few minutes Ben's confidence in his own judgment was shaken, and again he wished Gaucho were there. If he could just talk to Gaucho— He put his hand down on Peck's neck. It was warm and Ben wondered whether there had actually been a tremor or he had just imagined it. He hesitated a few seconds, then turned Peck toward the big longeing corral.

"If I'm wrong, Peck," he said, "there's plenty of time to find it out."

## ◄• *Fifteen* •►

They had been at the Andy Blair place ten days and Peck once again was coming along nicely when Andy asked Ben and Dixie if they would like to go to a place in California with him and Mrs. Blair to attend a running horse sale and a small race meet.

"Sure," Dixie said. "I'd love to go."

Ben was anxious to go too, but he was somewhat uncertain about leaving Peck. "That will be all right," Andy said. "I'll have Fred take him out every day and give him some exercise, just enough to limber up his legs. You really should see a sale; it might give you an idea of what kind of price you can expect for Peck."

They were gone three days. Andy Blair bought a new brood mare whose breeding he liked, and Ben didn't find any horses among the offerings which he thought were as good as Peck. The buyers backed his judgment by not bidding very strongly either.

"Jeez, Ben," Dixie whispered to him during the sale. "If we can't get more than this, we'll come out in the hole."

It was a poor sale, and discouraging to a boy and girl who would have a horse for sale later on. But the race meet was better, with some close and exciting finishes, and on the whole it was a pleasant and interesting trip for Ben and Dixie.

Back at the farm, however, things did not go smoothly. They learned, when they returned, that Troy Lane was in the hospital.

"What happened to him?" Andy Blair asked.

"Horse threw him," Fred said. "He has some ribs broken, and possibly other injuries."

"Is it serious?" Mrs. Blair asked.

"The doctor doesn't think so," Fred said. "But he should stay in the hospital a week or longer. It will probably be some time before he can ride again."

"And just when I need him most," Andy Blair said. "The sale is not a month away and the colts should be exercised regularly. Do you know anyone else we can get, Fred?"

The foreman shook his head.

"I'll do it," Dixie said earnestly. "I know how. Troy has shown me how to bring them along."

"Yes, but you'll need some help," Andy said. "There're too many for you to ride by yourself."

"I'll help her," Ben said. "I'll ride some of them."

"What about your own horse?" Andy asked.

"I can work him too," Ben said. "I'll have time, if Fred will help with the cooling out and grooming. I can get up earlier in the mornings if it's necessary."

"I'll help them, Mr. Blair," the foreman said. "I think we can handle it all right between us. Anyway I don't know of anyone else we can get right now."

"Well, all right, Ben, if you and Dixie will do it," Andy Blair said. "I didn't intend to put all this load on you, but I'll pay you."

"You don't have to," Ben said. "I want to do it. I don't know whether I can do as well as Troy, but I'll see that they get exercise."

"We'll do a good job," Dixie said confidently.

"And I want to pay you," Andy said. "Board and room, and the same wages Troy gets until he is back."

The days that followed were extremely busy ones for Ben and Dixie. Bright and early each morning, they were at the stables, saddling and readying young horses. Fred, on a saddle horse, would go with them past the big gate and help them mount into the light, short-stirruped training saddles. For a few mornings he went on to the track, to watch while they sent the colts around the oval in long canters. At first Ben tried to sit straight in the slick saddle, with reins held in one hand, as he was accustomed to galloping the ranch horses back at Tack. But the position, because of the short stirrups, was awkward and insecure.

Dixie quickly set him right. "Like this, Ben," she called. "They are trained to run against rein pressure, with the weight up front. Use your knees."

Ben saw that she had a rein in each hand and was leaning well forward over her horse's neck. He tried it. "But—you can't see anything," he said.

"You don't need to," she answered. "All a jockey needs to see is the track and the rail. You're not on a sightseeing bus." She grinned and added, "That's what Troy told me."

Ben found the position not as bad as he had imagined. By leaning forward like that, he could secure a grip on the horse's shoulders with his knees, and the steady pull of a rein in each hand added to his balance.

And he was amazed, too, by the way the young colt's stride smoothed out and became confident.

"That's it," Dixie told him. "Get your knees a little farther forward, and get your head lower. Ride from the stirrups. Don't let your weight interfere with the horse's action. Steady him with the reins, just enough to keep him smooth. There. That's better."

Ben was impressed. It was more work, much more, but it was easy to see how the position would help a horse to run. The weight was over the front legs, leaving the powerful driving muscles of the hind legs and back free. This was riding purely for speed, and before Ben was through with his first horse his cramped leg muscles caused him to remember that Andy Blair had called it "work." But he did find it interesting and exciting.

They worked four colts that morning, and two in the afternoon. Ben's thigh muscles were tired and his knees ached from the unaccustomed short stirrups. "Gee, Dix," he said as they dismounted from the last pair of colts, "I never knew you could cram so much riding into one day."

"You've ridden twelve hours at a stretch back home, more than once," Dixie reminded him with a grin.

"Yes, but that was easy," Ben said. "Then the horse was carrying me; now I feel like I've been carrying the horse."

Dixie headed for the house, declaring that she was going to soak in a hot shower before dinner.

"I've got to give Peck a little work first," Ben said.

He brought out the brown horse, bridled him quickly, and tossed up his own stock saddle. He led the horse about the area for a few minutes, then mounted. He was tired and still thinking about the thrill of riding the racing colts, but at once it came to him that something was wrong with Peck. The horse tossed his head, ground at the bit, and rolled his eyes backward.

"Whoa, Peck," Ben said. "What's the matter with you?"

But Peck continued to act excited. Ben swung down and checked his bridle and saddle. He could find nothing wrong with them, but he noticed that the sweat was beginning to break out in the curve of Peck's neck. The horse moved his feet about restlessly, unable to keep still.

"What's the matter, boy?" Ben asked, now thoroughly concerned. Peck almost seemed to be a dif-

ferent horse. Ben couldn't understand it. But something was the matter. Peck was nervous and excitable
again, almost as bad as ever. Ben knew a feeling of
bitter discouragement. It seemed that he was just
wasting his time. Peck apparently was one of those
horses that couldn't be cured. After all the months
of tireless and careful training, of slow riding on the
brush trails and after cattle, Peck hadn't forgotten
his experiences on the race track.

"I can't understand you, fella," Ben said, shaking his
head tiredly. And he felt hurt, for it seemed that the big
brown horse had lost all confidence, even in him.

He did not mount again, but led Peck about the
area until Dixie came from the house and waved. He
knew then that it was nearly time for dinner. He
unsaddled Peck before the tack room door, watered
him, and put him in his stall. He made sure that there
was grain in the box and hay in the rack before he left
for the house. He knew he was late, so he hurriedly
washed and combed his hair.

"Well, Ben, how do you like to exercise race
horses?" Andy Blair asked in the dining room.

"Fine," Ben said.

"It's different from ordinary riding," Andy said.

"Yes, sir," Ben said.

"Back at the ranch, we ride to go someplace or get some work done," Dixie said. "But here we ride to see how easy we can make it for them to run."

Andy Blair nodded. "The purpose," he said, "is to interfere with their natural balance and co-ordination as little as possible. All good horsemen do that to a certain extent, but only in racing is it so very important to get the weight forward, over the weight-carrying part of the horse, which is his front legs."

Ben nodded. At any other time conversation such as this would have interested him keenly, but tonight he didn't have much enthusiasm for anything that had to do with horses. Peck had let him down, had fooled him. Peck wasn't going to be the fine race horse he had been so sure about. Ben felt all helpless and miserable inside, but of course he couldn't say anything to Dixie or Mr. Blair. He couldn't say anything to anyone, but they would find out in time—everyone would. Gaucho would find out, too. And Pop. And Mom. And Uncle Wes.

Uncle Wes? How would he pay Uncle Wes? He figured that he and Dixie might come out about even on their board bill with Andy Blair, but he would have to manage some way to pay Uncle Wes. Inky? He just couldn't sell Inky. Inky was more than a horse; he was his "Christmas horse," caught out of the wild bunch for him by Pop and Steve and Gaucho and Johnny Horn. He couldn't sell Inky—not unless he just had to.

## ◄ • *Sixteen* • ►

The next morning Ben and Dixie were back at Andy Blair's racing colts. Ben didn't tell Dixie, but he considered this work now more important than ever. They caught and saddled two horses, took them through the big gate, down into the pasture, and galloped them about the oval. Hunched over their necks, they let them stretch in long ground-eating strides, but all the while holding them steady and well under a run. They were too young and immature yet for that exhausting and nerve-straining gait. Now they were merely getting exercise, learning to handle their long slender legs, building muscles and conformation that would show well in the sales ring. Now, just as a roping horse had to learn to stop and turn, these colts were learning to run, to spurn the earth with their round hoofs.

Galloping around the track, Ben found himself almost resenting the young thoroughbred between his knees. This horse was lucky. He was getting the kind of early training that Peck should have had, and didn't get. Peck never had work like this. He never had a chance to learn the pleasure of a good stiff gallop on a bright windless morning. All Peck had been taught was run—run till he was crazy, run till he was staggering, run till he was blind, run until the stick began to fall. That was all he knew. But, Ben told himself, that wasn't the fault of this colt, nor the fault of Andy Blair.

It was late in the afternoon when they finished with the colts that were to be exercised that day. Dixie headed for the house. Mrs. Blair was going to the city that night and had invited Dixie to go. She had invited Ben too, and the temptation was strong, for they would stay in for dinner and afterward go to a show.

Dixie paused and turned. "You coming, Ben?" she asked.

Ben shook his head. "Tell Mrs. Blair I can't go," he said. "I've got to give Peck some work."

He took Peck out of the stall and led him to the tack

room. He put on the bridle and saddle. But he hesitated to mount. He didn't have much heart for it. He knew Peck would start to tremble and sweat, and he didn't want to see it.

The foreman, Fred, was working in the area, and once he paused and looked at Ben with a peculiar expression on his face. Fred can't understand it either, Ben thought bitterly. No one could understand it, no one but Ben—and possibly Gaucho. In his pessimism, Ben was not even sure that Gaucho would understand. A horse like Peck was difficult to understand. Even Ben had been fooled, like Peck's previous owners. He remembered the old saying among horsemen that the best thing to do with some horses is to give them "a quick selling and forget them," and now he was beginning to realize the truth of it. Some horses simply weren't worth the time and trouble. And apparently Peck was one. But it wasn't easy to admit defeat and failure, not with that big debt to Uncle Wes staring him in the face. Somehow that would have to be paid, for he had pledged himself to do it.

Ben took Peck back to his stall and turned him in. He knew the horse had not had much exercise, but he was discouraged and he was tired. He went to the house and he and Andy Blair ate their dinner together in the breakfast nook of the kitchen.

"How'd the colts go today, Ben?" Andy asked. He never tired of talking about those young horses of his.

"Good," Ben said. "They're nice colts, Mr. Blair." And he couldn't keep the enthusiasm for them out of his voice when he said that.

Andy was visibly pleased. "I'm glad you think they're good," he said. "I do too. And you and Dixie are putting them in good shape. They're going to open the eyes of some fellows I know at the sales this fall."

"I hope they do," Ben said. "And I'm sure they will. If I had the money, there's one or two I would like to have myself."

"Well," Andy said thoughtfully, "I'm holding them pretty high. But your credit is good with me."

Ben shook his head and said, "No. I've got one horse on credit now, and that's enough for me."

"By the way," Andy asked, "how's your horse doing? I haven't seen you ride him much lately."

Ben lowered his eyes. He hated to admit it, but he said, "Not too good. He's not coming along like he should."

"I'm sorry to hear that," Andy said sincerely.

"What's the trouble? Don't you have enough time to work him?"

"Yes, it's not that," Ben said. "I — I don't know just what it is. He's a big strong horse, with lots of spirit, but he's not mean, and as much as I have ridden and worked him he should be all right. But he's not. Something is the matter with him."

"Still nervous and excitable?" Andy asked.

Ben nodded. "I can't figure it out. He seems to be coming along just fine, then all of a sudden he's right back where we started from. And for no reason, as far as I can tell."

"Some horses are like that, especially racers," Andy said sympathetically. "It gets so bad it's like a disease and they just can't control it. But most of them have a naturally mean streak in them."

"Peck doesn't," Ben said. "At least, I don't think he has."

"It happens to nearly everyone who has fooled around with horses much," Andy Blair said. "It has happened to me more often than I care to think about. But it's the ones that turn out good that you remember."

Ben was still thinking about Peck, and he shook his

head. "I can't understand it," he said. "He was coming along just fine."

"Maybe Fred can help us," Andy Blair said.

"I don't know," Ben said, without much hope.

"I'll call Fred," Andy said. "He's a good horseman, one of the best I know. He's been with horses all his life. If anyone knows, he should." Andy lifted the telephone and called the foreman's house.

Ben waited in silence, ready now to admit that he needed help and willing to take it anywhere he could get it. But he wasn't hopeful, for he believed he knew better than anyone else could possibly know the full size of his problem. The only man he knew who might help was Gaucho, and it was useless to think about that. He wouldn't take Peck back to Tack; he couldn't—not after Pop had given him so much time to devote to the horse. And he couldn't say that Pop hadn't warned him in the beginning. Pop had been the smart one. Ben wondered what he could do with Peck. Knowing what he knew, he would hesitate to offer him to anyone he liked as a gift.

There was a knock on the kitchen door and Fred Ward came in. He was a small man with big hands and a wiry body, and Ben knew that he, too, had once been a jockey. His hair was gray and his face was deeply tanned by the hot Arizona sun. There were deep wrinkles about his gray eyes. Now there was a sober, thoughtful expression on his face.

"Sit down, Fred," Andy Blair said in his easy, friendly manner. "We're just talking about horses."

Fred nodded and took a chair, holding his big hands interlocked between his knees.

"We've got a problem," Andy went on, "and we thought you might be able to help us with it."

"I will if I can," Fred said.

"I guess the big problem is to find someone who will take a spoiled race horse going on five years old," Ben said bitterly.

Andy Blair chose to overlook this outburst. "Ben's having trouble with his horse, Fred," Andy said. "He's nervous and excitable, and wants to run away. As you know, Ben has put in a lot of time and work on him, but he doesn't seem to be making much progress. We wondered if you might have some ideas?"

Fred Ward glanced down at his hands before he answered. "Yes, sir, Mr. Blair," he said presently, "I think I do. I've been aiming to tell you, but I just haven't done it. I guess maybe it's my fault."

"Your fault?" Andy said, with sharp surprise.

Ben looked up, wondering.

"Yes, sir," the foreman said. "When you went to California to that sale the other day, you told me to exercise Ben's horse. The Daisy mare foaled, and she was having some trouble, and I was pretty busy—and I told Troy. And I guess I didn't make it plain that he was to lead the horse."

"He rode him?" Ben cried.

Fred nodded unhappily.

"On the track?" Andy asked.

Again Fred nodded.

"That's what happened to him," Ben cried. "That's the reason he's been nervous and jumpy. That's it, Mr. Blair. That's it." And his voice was happy with relief. He knew now.

But Andy Blair was eyeing Fred sternly. "Peck's the horse that threw Troy?" he asked.

"Yes, sir," Fred said. "He ran away with him. Troy lost control of him."

"He knew better than to do that," Andy said angrily. "I should fire him."

"No," Ben said. "Don't fire him."

"But he spoiled all of your careful work," Andy said.

"Maybe he set it back some, but he hasn't spoiled it," Ben said. "I'm sure of that now."

"Do you think you can still bring Peck out of it?" Andy asked.

Ben nodded, renewed confidence bright in his eyes. "Yes, sir," he said. "I think I can."

# ◄• Seventeen •►

**B**en was so relieved at finding out what the trouble was with Peck that it wasn't in his heart to hold ill feeling against either Fred or Troy. Now that he knew what had happened, he knew what to do about it, and he went to work with a new determination. With Dixie, he continued to ride Andy Blair's colts, but also in the afternoon he devoted long hours to the big brown horse, leading him, riding him, and handling him.

"You're going to get over it, Peck," he said. "You're going to be a race horse yet."

And Peck did get over it, rapidly. With the careful handling, his confidence in Ben was soon restored. By degrees, Ben enlarged the scope of their riding. He took the horse into the pasture, rode him among the grazing mares and their foals, much as he had ridden him among the cattle back at Tack. He made this a part of the regular routine, and on the third afternoon even permitted the horse to gallop a short distance. The next day there was more galloping, and the day after that still more. Ben was elated; the brown horse was coming along. He galloped without fuss or excitement.

Then the afternoon came when Ben decided to make a still more tricky test, for he felt that Peck was ready for it. He rode the horse through the opening in the track fence. Peck raised his head and looked about, obviously looking for other horses. But there was none in sight, save the mares and foals grazing contentedly outside.

"Take it easy," Ben said. "There's no one here but us. No reason for you to get excited."

He rode around the track twice, but kept the horse at a walk all the time.

The next afternoon, he galloped Peck, but for only a short distance and on the back stretch. When pulled up, the horse tossed his head a bit, but Ben quickly calmed him.

Troy Lane came back from the hospital. He was pale, and rested most of the time, but his broken ribs had knitted nicely. "I'm sorry," he said to Ben, some-what shamefacedly. "I didn't aim to let him get away from me. I wasn't ready when he took off."

"That's all right," Ben said. He was sitting on the brown horse in the stable area then.

Troy looked at the horse and there was a suggestion of a shaking of his head. "He took the bit in his teeth and I couldn't hold him," he said. "I was afraid he was going to hit the fence."

Ben realized that Troy did not think much of his chances of curing the horse, but Peck was doing so well that Ben was in no mood to argue. He merely nodded his head and said, "I know."

And he knew, too, that Troy Lane might be right, for the big test was yet to come. Ben prepared for it carefully. Every afternoon, alone in the deepening twi-light, he worked the horse on the track, alternately gal-loping and walking him. He let him gallop until he showed signs of wanting to run; then he made him walk until he was calm again. Sometimes he would take him out and gallop him among the feeding mares, turning him frequently to keep his mind on his business and make him watch where he was going. Then he would bring him back to the track for a slow gallop. At the stables he led him until he was thoroughly dry and cool. Fred offered to do this cooling for him, since it was often well after dark before Ben could finish and go to the house for dinner. But Ben shook his head. This was something he had to do himself, and he never failed to water the horse and see that he had grain and hay before he went for his own meal. Peck was coming along. Ben knew he was, and he was determined nothing should spoil it.

Troy Lane started working the colts again, riding with Dixie. Ben was pleased, for it gave him more time with Peck. He rode and worked the brown horse, galloping him mile after mile in the pasture and around the track.

"He's sure got stamina," Fred said one morning as he helped Ben nail on a new set of light steel shoes.

"He sure has," Ben agreed.

"He's in top condition," Fred said. "That helps. But you'd better keep after him or he'll get too frisky."

"I expect to," Ben said.

And he did. Time after time he brought Peck back to his stall really weary, believing there was nothing like plain old-fashioned tiredness to relieve high-tension nerves. Peck forgot he was a prima donna, bred and trained for those few screaming seconds of pandemonium on the race track. He began to realize that the day had a morning as well as an afternoon and both could be filled with work. Energy became something too important to waste uselessly.

One afternoon Ben said, "Catch a horse, Dixie, not one of the colts, and come down to the track. I want you to help me."

The time had come to put Peck in company, and Ben well realized that this was a stronger test than any to which he had put the brown horse previously. This was the thing which heretofore had proved Peck's undoing.

Ben had limbered Peck up at a walk and had made one circle of the track at a brisk canter when Dixie appeared, riding Mrs. Blair's gentle Sunday.

"Come on the track and ride around," Ben called to her. "Don't pay any attention to me and be sure not to let Sunday run."

Peck raised his head and nickered at the sight of the new horse. "No you don't," Ben said firmly, and with reins and heels brought the horse's attention back to the business at hand. Peck galloped on, but at another hundred yards he raised his head and looked back over his shoulder. "Get along," Ben said, jabbing sternly with his heels.

Peck went on. Ben passed Dixie's loafing horse, and

again Peck showed interest. When Ben straightened him, he attempted to break into a run. "No you don't," Ben said, pulling back strongly. Peck settled into his canter. "Turn around and go the other way," Ben called back to Dixie.

The next time the two horses met they were moving in opposite directions, Peck at a hard gallop and Sunday at a walk. Peck tried to stop and turn, to go in the same direction as Dixie. Ben straightened him out and sent him on. "Okay," he yelled to Dixie. "That's enough."

Dixie left the track and went back to the stables. Ben galloped Peck two more rounds, until the horse was content with a loose rein. Then, with voice alone, he slowed Peck to a walk. "Good horse, Peck, good horse," he said, pleased. The brown stallion had withstood the test.

But other and more difficult tests were coming. This had been merely company, not actual racing. Any of Andy Blair's colts would have behaved themselves equally as well, if not better. Nevertheless Ben was elated; Andy Blair's colts had not been spoiled.

Ben went at Peck with more determination than ever. Work, work, work. He never in those days pulled off the saddle until the horse showed definite signs of being tired. He never pulled off the saddle until Peck was willing to stand, head down and quiet.

"If riding will do it, you'll win," Fred told him one afternoon as he stood at the trough by the drinking Peck.

Ben was pleased, but he didn't permit himself to do more than nod his head and say, "That's the way I figure it."

Dixie was riding with him every afternoon these days, riding Sunday or some other gentle horse. She rode about the track, turning and stopping, even galloping occasionally while Ben worked Peck. And Ben took care to keep Peck too busy with his own movements to pay attention to the other horse.

Dixie was highly encouraged. "He's coming along, Ben," she said. "You've got him in hand."

Ben decided to make another test. "Put your horse in a gallop behind me," he said to Dixie, and went on along the track.

The pound of hoofs back there caused Peck's ears to swivel around and almost instinctively he reached for greater distance with his front feet. "No," Ben said and pulled the horse down firmly.

They went this way until Peck was galloping free again, then Ben called, "Speed up and pass me."

The rhythm of the hoofbeats behind increased, and came nearer. Once again Peck showed excitement, and once again his long front legs reached out. "Easy, easy," Ben said and forced the horse back to a canter. Peck fretted a bit as Dixie approached them, but Ben held him steady. He fretted still more as Dixie went away from them and tried to line out in pursuit. But Ben held him in.

"Breeze him," Ben yelled at Dixie, using the term that they had picked up from the running-horse men.

Dixie let her horse stretch into a run and the hoof sound became a steady drumming as they went on around the track. Peck fought for the bit. But Ben was ready. "Oh, no," Ben said. He pulled the horse down and, after a second or two, let him resume the steady galloping. Peck put up his head and watched the horse around in the stretch, but he did not try to bolt again. Presently Ben pulled him down to a walk and Dixie, at a slow trot now, came on around.

She reined her horse in beside Peck and said, "He did swell. Even the colts would have wanted to run then."

Ben nodded his head. He was pleased. Also he was cautious. "He hasn't raced yet," he said.

"He will, any time now," Dixie declared.

"Not till I'm sure he's ready," Ben said.

And a few days later he was sure. He brought Peck up beside Sunday and said, "Let 'em stretch, Dix."

Dixie shook the reins in her horse's ears and Sunday lined out, so quickly that Ben was momentarily left behind. But Peck, freed at last to do the thing he loved most, quickly caught up, and Ben held him steady in a neck and neck position with Sunday along the back stretch. They stepped at a good gait. Peck wanted to really stretch, but Ben held him in. Dixie grinned and nodded. Ben thrilled with pleasure, for he knew that Dixie could see that Peck was under perfect control.

"He's all right," Dixie said, a short time later when they pulled up. "He handles as good as any horse. He's ready to sell."

"You think so?" Ben asked, not certain himself.

"Sure," Dixie said. "Do you realize that the summer is almost over? We'll have to be going back to Idaho pretty soon, to start to school. There's not much time left."

"Say," Ben said, with sudden realization and some concern, "that's right."

# ◄• Eighteen •►

**D**ixie and Troy Lane were riding two of Andy Blair's racing colts toward the track in the pasture the next afternoon when Ben caught up with them. Troy saw that Ben was riding Peck and his eyes opened with some surprise. "You going with us, Ben?" he asked.

Ben nodded. "I think he's ready for company."

"We breeze them around pretty fast," Troy said, as a warning.

"That's all right," Ben said. "Don't pay any attention to me."

They didn't. Ben let Peck watch the running colts awhile before he put him on the track. The colts were on the back stretch and Ben held Peck to a gallop, warming him slowly. Dixie and Troy took their colts back to the stables. Ben pulled Peck down and let him walk. Dixie and Troy came back presently, with two fresh colts. They walked them awhile, then galloped them, and when they did Ben galloped beside them. After a warming round, they let the young horses stretch, and Ben let Peck stretch too, let him really run, and he moved out in front immediately.

"Well," Troy said, when they had pulled up, "you couldn't ask for a nicer-handling horse."

"He's all right," Dixie said. "I keep telling Ben that. We've got to sell him before it's time for us to go back to Idaho."

"How much do you want for him?" Troy said. "I'd buy him, if I had the money."

"We'll have to get a good price," Ben said.

"We've got a note to pay, and a big feed bill," Dixie said. "And," she went on, wrinkling her freckled nose, "some insurance. That was my idea."

"Maybe Mr. Blair will buy him," Troy said. "He might. Do you want me to find out for you?"

"Sure," Dixie said. "We've got to sell him."

But Ben shook his head. "I don't know," he said. "I wouldn't want Mr. Blair to buy him—not unless he really wanted him. Do you understand what I mean? This is strictly a business deal."

"I know," Troy said, nodding. "But Mr. Blair might want him. He's a better horse than I thought he was. I'll find out for you. I can do it easy like, without asking him right out."

"All right," Dixie agreed.

"But don't tell him we brought it up," Ben said.

Dixie turned on him and said, "We owe Uncle Wes three hundred dollars, and twenty-five more for insurance. I hope you haven't forgotten that."

"I haven't," Ben said. "I can't forget it," he added with a grimace. "But I don't want Mr. Blair to buy him just as a favor to us."

"All right, hard-head," Dixie said. "I don't either. But I hope he wants him. We haven't got much time left."

"I'll find out," Troy promised.

It was the next morning before Troy had anything to tell them. He shrugged his shoulders unhappily and shook his head. "I mentioned it to him," he said. "I told him Peck was a good horse—a plumb good running horse. But he didn't bite. He's not interested."

"Jeez," said Dixie, disappointed.

And Ben was disappointed too, despite his objections on the previous day. He had secretly hoped that

Andy Blair would want the horse. Now he had difficulty in hiding his chagrin.

"I'm sorry," Troy Lane said. "If I had the money, I'd buy him myself. He'll win some races."

"That's all right, Troy," Ben said.

"Well," Dixie said exasperatedly, "what are we going to do now? Where do we go from here?"

"We'll give him some more work," Ben said.

"Work!" Dixie exclaimed. "What else can you do with him?"

"There's one more thing," Ben said. "There's one more thing, and it's important."

"Well, for goodness sakes, what is it?" Dixie said.

"Someone else has to ride him," Ben said slowly, for this was something that he had been evading for a long time. "I can't ride him in any races. He's got to get used to other people. See what I mean?"

"I do," Troy Lane said. "He's got to be so a jockey can ride, any jockey."

"That's right," Ben said, then added by way of correction, "any good jockey."

Troy Lane's rugged face turned a bit red and he said, "I'll admit I figured him wrong. I thought I could handle him."

"Oh, I didn't mean that," Ben said quickly. "He ran

away with me too, the first time I was on his back. But I know him now. I can ride him, but someone else will have to too."

There was a short silence, then Troy Lane said, "I'd like to try him, if you think I can, Ben. I'll handle him careful. If he can get used to me, that'll be something. It won't be so hard then for someone else."

"Sure," Dixie said. "Troy can ride him. Let Troy ride him. That'll help."

But Ben still hesitated.

"I know I let him run away once, Ben," the jockey said soberly, "but I don't think it'll happen again."

"All right," Ben said. "I believe you can do it."

But he wouldn't let Troy take Peck to the track at first. He made him ride him around the stables and in the big training corral. He had him feed him and groom him, and water him and do all the handling, until he was certain that the horse knew the jockey and had confidence in him. Troy, remembering that he had once sadly underestimated Peck, accepted all this in good spirit. He worked with Peck as Ben had worked with him, while Ben spelled him on Mr. Blair's colts.

Ben watched all this with a keen eye, and with some doubts at first. But gradually he became more assured. "What about it?" he asked Troy one morning.

"I've got him," the jockey said. "There won't be any trouble."

"You should know by now," Ben said. "Bring him out to the track."

Ben rode a colt right beside Peck on that trial run. Troy was riding a racing saddle, his knees high up. Dixie was on the other side, riding the pretty sorrel filly. They went around, holding their horses well in. Ben saw that Troy, well forward, balanced the big horse nicely.

"How's he going?" Ben asked.

"Nice," Troy said, without taking his eyes from Peck's ears.

"All right," Ben said. "Let 'em stretch." He leaned forward and low on his own horse.

"Hi, hi," Troy said, and the big brown horse, running smoothly and easily, began to pull away from the colts.

"Scat!" Dixie yelled into the sorrel's ears. Like Troy, she was well forward and low.

Ben let his horse out another notch, too. But still the big brown pulled away from them. They rounded the turn and Troy had no trouble holding Peck steady past the open track gate, where even a lot of the best-trained horses show hesitancy. They went on, into the next turn, Peck laying close into the rail and Ben and Dixie pounding behind him.

Then Troy deliberately pulled the big horse in. "Whoa. Whoa, Peck," he said and tightened the reins. Peck began to slow down.

"Keep going," Ben called to Dixie. They galloped on past the brown horse. He reared and lunged, anxious to run, but Troy quickly and easily brought him under control.

Ben pulled up and he and Dixie turned their sweating colts. "What do you think?" Ben asked Troy, a bit anxiously.

"I can handle him," Troy said confidently. "Sure he's high; he wouldn't be a race horse if he wasn't. But any good jockey should be able to get along with him."

"Good," Ben said. "That's what I've been working for. He's a good horse, Troy."

"He sure is," the jockey answered. "He's got as nice a stride as any horse I ever rode. He really reaches out."

"He sure does," Ben said. "I wish Gaucho were here. I wish he could see him now."

"I do too," Dixie said. "And I wish I could see Gaucho. And Mom and Pop."

"Let's take them in," Ben said. "They've had

enough." He knew that Dixie was homesick for Tack, that she was thinking about getting back to Idaho. And he was too. But they couldn't go yet.

Dixie brought the subject up again that night after they had finished dinner. She came to Ben's room and said, "Do you realize that it's less than two weeks until school starts in Boise?"

"No," Ben said, unbelievingly.

"It is," Dixie said. "We've got to start thinking about going home."

"We can't, not until we've sold Peck," Ben said.

"We'll have to," Dixie said. "You know well enough that Pop won't let us stay and miss school. We've got to find some buyers. We'll have to have some money when we get back, to pay Uncle Wes."

Several seconds passed before Ben answered. Then he said, "Yes, I guess we'll have to. But jeez, Dix, I don't know how to sell him—not now."

"Show him," Dixie said. "You've got to let somebody look at him."

"All right," Ben said but still reluctantly. "Let's go see Mr. Blair."

Andy Blair was in the living room, with his wife. He looked up from his paper as Ben and Dixie came in.

"I think my horse is all right now, Mr. Blair," Ben said.

Andy nodded. "I knew he was coming along," he said. "Troy tells me you've done a good job on him."

"I need to sell him, to a good owner," Ben said. "I thought maybe you might know of somebody who would buy him."

"We haven't much time," Dixie said. "We'll have to be going back to Idaho pretty soon now. School starts."

"We have good schools here," Mrs. Blair said with a smile.

Dixie smiled back at her but shook her head. "We'll have to go back to Idaho," she said.

"Say, there's a sale next Tuesday," Andy Blair said, suddenly remembering. "It's a sale and a one-day race meet. Would you like to go? We can take Peck. There'll be some buyers there. It might be a chance to sell him."

But Ben wasn't thinking about the sale. "A race meet?" he said. "Could we let Peck run? Could we do that, Mr. Blair?"

"Why, yes, I suppose so," Andy said. "Are you sure you want to enter him in a race? Who'll ride him?"

"Troy," Ben said. "Troy will ride him."

# ◄•*Nineteen*•►

*T*hey went to a track in southern California, where a running-horse sale was being held. And as a special attraction to draw buyers there was a one-day race meet, with some good horses entered. The fourth race was for a mile, all the way around the big oval, and that suited Ben, for that was the distance Peck liked. He had the stamina and the heart for it.

Ben was standing around in front of Peck's stall, as nervous as a cat, though Troy Lane assured him that the big horse was in top condition. "He's right," Troy said, and Troy should have known, for he himself had put the final touches to Peck's training. But still Ben was nervous. "Aw," Troy told him finally, "you're worse than Peck used to be."

"I can't help it," Ben said.

Andy and Mrs. Blair and Dixie had walked away somewhere, but a number of people were moving about in the stable area. Ben knew that some of them were buyers. Now and then one stopped to look at Peck. Several asked questions about him. Practically all the horses there were for sale.

Andy and Mrs. Blair and Dixie came back. Dixie was full of excitement. "Ben, you should see the good mare Mr. Blair just bought," she said. "She's a beauty."

A well-dressed man in a gray suit and carrying a walking stick had been looking at Peck. "Is this horse for sale?" he asked gruffly.

"Yes, sir," Ben said.

"How much?" the man asked.

"Well, I haven't put a price on him yet," Ben said. "Not till after the race. He's in the fourth."

"Humpf," the man said and moved on.

Dixie shook her head. "You're leading with your chin," she told Ben. "After the race maybe nobody will want him."

"I think they will," Ben said. "I think they'll want him all right."

And Troy Lane backed him. "Don't you worry,

Ben," Troy said. Troy was wearing his faded old racing silks, cap, and shirt. He had on white breeches and short, black, flat-heeled boots.

Andy Blair grinned and said, "I guess that's the way I'd do it, Ben. I like to see a man have confidence in his horse."

"But you don't owe Uncle Wes three hundred dollars," Dixie said. "And a feed bill to Pop. And a board bill to Andy Blair. If Peck doesn't sell, I don't know how we'll even get back to Idaho."

Andy laughed at her. "You can go back to Arizona and work for me," he said. He turned to Ben. "How much are you going to ask for your horse, Ben?"

"I don't know yet," Ben said. "All I can get. What would you say would be a good price?"

"If he wins, or if he loses?" Andy asked thoughtfully.

"If he wins," Ben said.

"A thousand—maybe twelve hundred," Andy said. "Of course, it will depend a lot on how he goes. If he looks really good, someone might go a little higher."

"And if he loses?" Dixie said.

Andy shrugged and said, "That's hard to say. But it won't be as much, probably by quite a bit. It would be different if he had outstanding breeding."

Another well-dressed man was approaching the stall.

"Sell him," Dixie whispered to Ben fiercely. "Sell him if he makes you a decent offer."

The man stopped, eyed the horse. "Would you mind bringing him out?" he asked presently.

"No, sir," Ben said. He snapped a rope in Peck's halter ring and led him out of the stall. The man moved about him, his head bent critically to one side.

But before he could say anything else, another man arrived, a tall raw-boned man in a cheap, wrinkled blue suit. This second man stopped and stared, as if he couldn't believe his eyes. "That—that's Peck," he said, gulping. "That's Peck o' Trouble."

"Yes," Ben said, eyeing this stranger closely. "You know him?"

"Know him?" the man boomed in a voice that could be heard all over the area. "I bred and raised him. I put the first saddle on his back. I gave him that blasted name."

"You did?" Ben cried in amazement.

"I sure did," the man replied. "Say, what're you doing with him here? He can't be ridden on a race track. He's been ruled off of all the tracks in Idaho and eastern Oregon."

Ben frowned and turned to look at the first man. This man gave a knowing little smile, shook his head, and turned away, not interested any more.

But Dixie didn't even notice. "Idaho?" she cried at the raw-boned man. "Are you from Idaho?"

"Sure am, miss," the man boomed. "Owyhee country. Best horse country in the world."

"Owyhee!" Ben said. "Did you ever hear of Tack Ranch, or Vince Darby?"

"Sure have," the man said. "I live over Grandview way myself, but I've heard of the Darby outfit. On Crystal Creek, ain't it?"

"I'm Ben Darby," Ben said. "Vince is my dad. And this is my sister, Dixie." Ben was so glad to see someone from home that he couldn't hold it against the man for ruining a possible sale.

"Well, what do you know!" the man said, putting out his hand. "I'm Lige Singleton."

Ben introduced him to Andy and Mrs. Blair, and to Troy Lane.

"It seems to be a small world," Andy Blair said, smiling.

"It sure does," Lige Singleton said. "I'm down here looking for some good running prospects. Can't get over fooling with race horses. I've had some good ones too. But say," he went on to Ben, "what's Peck doing here?"

"I'm going to sell him," Ben said. "I brought him here to sell."

Lige Singleton waggled his hands in the air above his head. "Not me," he cried, as if fearful of the very thought. "Not to me. That horse nigh drove me crazy. He's the headstrongest horse I ever saw. You wouldn't believe it—ran away with every boy I put on his back. Oh no, don't sell him to me."

Ben smiled and said, "He's not like that now."

"I'll have to see it to believe it," Lige said in a shout, which seemed to be his normal voice.

"Just wait till the fourth race," Troy Lane said.

"Here comes Fred," Andy Blair said. "Ben, you and Dixie, maybe we had better be getting to the grand-stand. The races will start in a few minutes now. Would you like to come with us, Mr. Singleton? I have a box."

"Well—yes," Lige Singleton said. "If you're sure you have room, Mr. Blair."

The first race was a good one, a big bay horse win-ning by half a length. But Ben was too excited to pay much attention. He kept thinking about Peck. The second race was slow.

"I've got an old saddle horse that can run faster than that," Lige Singleton said with some disgust.

The third race, a half mile for two-year-olds, was fast and close, bringing everyone in the box except Ben up to his feet. While the winner was coming back, Ben said, "Maybe I'd better go. They may need some help with Peck."

Andy Blair shook his head and said, "Don't worry, Ben. Fred is there with Troy. They'll have him ready."

Ben sat down in his chair again, and just at that instant Andy Blair jumped up from his. "Vince," Andy called to a man coming along the aisle. "I was afraid you weren't going to make it in time."

"Just got here," said a hearty voice that fairly lifted Ben to his feet.

"Pop!" Dixie shrieked, whirling up so quickly that she upset her chair. "And Mom! And Uncle Wes! And Gaucho! Oh, oh, oh—" She danced up and down with happiness and excitement. "And Aunt Mary, too!"

Ben almost fell over himself getting to them. "How'd you know?" he cried. "How'd you know, Mom?"

"A little bird told us," Vince said, winking broadly at Andy Blair.

"A big bird, Ben," Mrs. Blair said, nodding her head to confirm Ben's suspicion.

"We'd have been here sooner," Pop said, "but we got lost. I hope we didn't miss the race."

"I do too," Uncle Wes said. "I've got a special interest in this race, at six percent," he went on, winking at Ben.

"You've missed three of them," Dixie said. "Gee, it seems like all of Idaho is here. This is Mr. Lige Singleton—Mom and Pop. He's from Idaho too."

"Owyhee country, same as you," Lige Singleton boomed. "I'm over near Grandview, but I've heard about your Tack Ranch over on Crystal Creek. I'm down here to see if I can pick up a good running prospect. Been fooling with race horses all my life. Can't get 'em out of my blood."

"Has our horse run yet, Ben?" Milly asked anxiously.

"Not yet, Mom," Ben said.

"He's in the next race," Andy Blair said. "Here, Milly, sit here beside May. You too, Aunt Mary—I've heard about you. Gaucho, get up there beside Ben. Vince and I will sit back here. You there, Mr. Singleton."

"They should be bringing them out pretty quick now," Andy Blair said, looking toward the track entrance. "It's about time. A jockey that works for me is up on Ben's horse. He's a good rider."

"Ben's horse?" Dixie said, wrinkling her nose at him. "How often do I have to tell you that half of that horse belongs to me? A woman sure has to stick up for her rights with a horse."

## ◄•*Twenty*•►

"*T*here! there, Gaucho! That's him out there—in the purple and gold."

The horses were coming onto the track for the fourth. Led by a race official on a pinto chubby by comparison, they came through the gate in single file, a line of sleek thoroughbreds mounted by jockeys in bright colored shirts and caps. They turned right, to parade down before the packed grandstand and back before the start.

"I see Peck already," Gaucho said proudly. "Looking good, Ben."

"I hope so, I hope so," Ben chanted in his excitement.

"That's him there, Pop," Dixie said, pointing. "Hold

him tight, Troy," she yelled at the jockey.

The horses pranced on past. The man on the pinto went out the gate and off the track, leaving the starter in charge. At the starter's signal the jockeys turned their horses and began maneuvering for position and advantage, not knowing of course what instant the flag would come down.

"That Peck will never start," Lige Singleton muttered half unconsciously to himself.

Tension in the horses noticeably increased as the riders sought to bring them to instant readiness and keep them there. There was turning and milling, with the jockeys dividing their attention between their horses and the starter. Ben couldn't take his eyes from the scene. Peck had drawn the third position in a field of six horses and was between a bay and a gray. The gray was a bad one, half out of control. He kept lunging and rearing, so close to Peck that Ben's heart climbed up into his throat. Excitement is contagious among horses and Ben didn't know whether Peck could stand that.

But the rider out there on the brown horse's back wasn't missing a trick. With voice and hand he soothed the horse, holding him firmly but not too tightly, giving rein now and then for a nerve-relieving stretch of the long neck, turning him, keeping him in position and keeping those long flat muscles coiled. Out of the corner of his eye he watched the gray and avoided the lunges. There was a break, an instant of loosened reins and driving legs, but the starter yelled, "No, no," and waved the flag negatively above his head.

The jockeys sought to calm and quiet the horses on the way back to the line, taking their time. There was prancing and turning and pulling at the reins as once more they maneuvered for positions. Hips and shoulders collided as the line thickened and crowded. The gray reared, straight up for a breathless second, then came back to the earth with stiff, jarring legs.

Ben's own agony was expressed in a groaned "Oh," and he only half realized that it came from Lige Singleton, who was watching with wide staring eyes.

The horses milled and turned again. Troy Lane was cool and watchful, alert and holding to his position. They were in line, heads for once all turned the same way. The starter seized the opportunity, bringing his flag down with a mighty flourish. A piercing yell went up from the stands and the six thoroughbreds were in flight. Ben, as everyone else, was on his feet.

It was a ragged start, the first three horses bunched

hard on the rail and the other three scattered behind. Peck was among the first three, Ben quickly saw. In the lead, tight against the rail, there was a big bay, bright and beautiful in the smooth sweep of his stride. Behind him was Peck, and beside Peck, on the outside, was the troublesome gray, who by some good luck had gotten away to a good start. It was difficult to tell whether Peck or the gray was in front. In this position, they swept around the turn.

"Come on, Peck, come on!" Dixie screamed jumping up and down excitedly.

The horses streamed on, into the back stretch, and there the onlookers had opportunity to see clearly the fine rhythmic stride of the brown. His long legs moved with sure power; his neck was outstretched and Troy Lane's gold cap was close above the dark mane. But the big bay in the lead was mighty and confident, and the gray outside still ran strong.

"They've got him trapped," Andy Blair said, discontent in his voice. "I don't like that."

"Come on, Peck. Go, boy," Mrs. Blair cried.

Along the back stretch they flew, the first three horses still together in a tight knot, but distance now opening between the others. The race was between the three leaders, and their relative positions remained unchanged as they passed the three-quarters post and went into the far turn.

"How long can that gray keep it up?" Andy Blair fumed.

"Don't worry," tall Lige Singleton said without clear meaning.

The horses flew around the end of the track and swept into the stretch. Everyone in the stands was up and shouting. From this head-on view they could see the bay and the gray, coming with reaching, pounding feet. Peck was somewhere behind them, back in that ruck of bobbing heads and flying manes.

"Come on, Peck," Vince Darby's big voice boomed from behind Ben.

"Peck, Peck," Dixie screamed.

"Get out of that box," Andy Blair yelled. "Get him out of there, Troy."

"Come on, come on," Milly Darby cried.

"Don't worry," Lige Singleton said again.

And then it happened. Into that narrow space between the bay and the gray a dark head appeared. It drove in like an opening wedge, bold and determined, carrying the gray wide. A bobbing gold cap was above it. A dark form showed up. Then there were three horses, bay, brown and gray, running, it seemed, neck and neck, with the finish less than an eighth of a mile away.

The stands went wild, men and women screaming hysterically for their favorites.

"Peck! Come on, Peck," Ben shouted.

"Come on, Peck!" Vince's heavy voice pleaded.

"Come on. Come on," Andy Blair cried.

"You don't have to worry," Lige Singleton said, no one paying any attention to him in the excitement.

Now they could see that the gray was losing ground. His jockey was urging him with bat and heel, but it was no use. Peck and the bay pulled away from him, Peck outside and the bay on the rail. On they came, two big, game, beautiful horses, pounding, reaching, straining. Peck gained, came up, and for an instant they were neck and neck. The rider on the bay was using his bat, screaming at his horse. Troy Lane's face was grim and fixed, but Ben could see that he never said a word and he wasn't carrying a whip. And big Peck came on, came on gallantly, gamely, strong yet with reserve. He swept under the wire, winner by a full length, going away, easily the best horse on the track.

Ben became aware that someone was pounding him jubilantly on the back. It was Andy Blair. "We won, Ben, we won," Andy cried delightedly. "What do you think about that, Vince? What do you think about your boy as a horse trainer now?"

Ben looked at his mother. Her eyes sparkled with happy tears.

"He surprised me," Vince told Andy Blair simply. "I didn't think he could do it."

Troy Lane had halted Peck and was bringing him back. A wave of applause swept over the stands. The brown horse pranced proudly.

"Look at him, Ben," Dixie said. "Look at him. He's bowing to the people."

"The winnah!" a voice boomed over the loudspeaker system. "The winnah!"

The stands became suddenly quiet, and Andy Blair said, "Listen. Listen to this."

"The winnah," the announcer repeated, "is Peck o' Trouble, owned by Ben and Dixie Darby, trained by Ben Darby, ridden by Troy Lane."

"Ben! Oh, wow, Ben!" Dixie cried, grabbing at her brother's shoulder as she jumped up and down in happiness.

Ben was too filled with relief and joy to talk.

"That's one good job you did," Gaucho said to him in a low voice. "One good horse, too."

"Shucks," Lige Singleton shouted in his big Idaho voice. "I knew there wasn't no need to worry, not after he started. That horse always could run."

# ◄• *Twenty-One* •►

They went to the stables, Milly, Mrs. Blair, Uncle Wes, Gaucho, and all of them. There were more races to come, but what could they matter, after that glorious fourth? Troy Lane was squatted near the stall's open door, dirty and tired, but with a big joyful grin on his flushed face. A dozen yards away Fred Ward led the blanketed Peck in slow cooling circles.

"How'd he do, Troy? Was he all right?" Ben asked eagerly.

"Great," the jockey said. "He never faltered all the way, and when I asked for a finish—well, you saw it. He ran their legs off."

"That horse always could run," Lige Singleton said. "His only trouble was starting. How'd you do it, boy?"

Ben went over to the brown horse and rubbed his soft nose. "You're a swell horse, Peck," he said with warm feeling.

Lige Singleton cleared his throat loudly. "Maybe I'm crazy, folks," he said. "I've been accused of it. I swore once I'd never have that horse again, not even if somebody offered him to me as a gift under a four-hundred-dollar saddle. But if I remember right, Ben, you said you were going to sell him."

Ben looked up, hesitated, then resumed rubbing the horse's nose.

Vince Darby spoke. "A cow ranch is not much of a place for a race horse, Ben, especially a good one, but if you want to keep him—well, I reckon Tack can manage to support one."

"What about that note to Uncle Wes?" Dixie asked pointedly.

"Now don't worry about that," Uncle Wes said. "It's not pressing, and I don't think it ever will be."

"We can manage that too," Vince said. "I'll take it over, and you two can work it off at the ranch."

"There's a two-hundred-and-fifty-dollar purse for the race," Andy Blair reminded them. "Don't forget that."

Vince nodded and said, "That's right, Ben. We can manage, if you want to keep him."

"Oh, Ben, we can take him back to Idaho with us," Dixie said.

Ben shook his head. "He's too good a race horse for a ranch," he said. "He belongs on the tracks, where he can show what he can do."

"You're absolutely right," Lige Singleton said heartily. "He's a running horse. Put a price on him, son. Don't make it too high, and I'll take him back to Idaho."

Ben left the horse, so Fred could continue leading him. "Say, Mr. Singleton," he said, "I've been intending to ask you. You raised Peck. What about his sire—Big Trouble?"

"Not a bad horse," Lige said. "He was a good-looker, but he couldn't run too fast."

"Did you own him?" Ben asked.

"For a while I did, but not very long," Lige said. "To tell you the truth, he didn't do too good. Only won one race for me."

"Was he a big horse?"

"Medium, just medium," the man said.

"Where do you think Peck got his size?" Ben asked.

"Dogged if I know," Lige said. "He just grew big—big and wild. You should have seen him when he was a colt."

"You live in the Grandview country," Ben said. "Did you ever hear of Twin Buttes?"

"Sure. Sure I have," Lige said. "Have run horses over there, wild ones. Had to go over there after some of my own, more'n once. They'd get out, and them wild studs would run them off, 'specially the mares. They'd take them to heck and gone. I've got a good race mare up there now; don't reckon I'll ever catch her."

"Did you ever see King?" Dixie asked.

"King?" Lige repeated.

"A black stallion," Ben explained, "the leader of the biggest bunch."

"Oh, him? Sure I've seen him, but from a distance," Lige said. "You can't get close to that horse. He's the wildest thing I ever saw, not barrin' buck deer."

A man approached the group, the man in the gray suit who had been there earlier in the afternoon. "That horse for sale?" he asked, nodding toward Peck.

But Ben was too intent to talk to him. Ben didn't take his eyes from Lige Singleton's face. "What about Miss Peck?" Ben said. "Did she ever get out?"

Vince Darby frowned and said, "There's a man that might want to buy your horse, Ben."

"Hush, Vince," his wife said. She was as intent as Ben on what Lige Singleton had to say.

"Well, now, let's see," Lige said, thinking. "Yes, come to think of it, she did. Once. She was gone about two weeks, as I recollect. But I didn't have any trouble with her. She was gentle, easy as pie to catch. Was plumb up near Little Butte Springs, though. That's one time I saw the black stallion—when I was up there after the Miss. She was the best—"

"When was it? How long ago?" Ben asked eagerly.

"Heck, I don't know. A long time. Three or four years," Lige said.

"When was it? Think back," Ben said. "I've got to know."

"Before Miss Peck—before she had her foal?" Gaucho asked, his dark eyes wide with wonderment.

"Dogged if I remember," Lige said. "It was quite a spell."

"What difference does that make, Ben?" Vince said impatiently.

Milly silenced him with a sharp dig of her elbow. Like Gaucho, she knew what was in Ben's mind.

"Five years?" Ben shot the question at Lige.

"Well, let's see," the man said. "It was while I had Big Trouble; I recollect that. I figured first I might ride him when I went to look for her, then I thought better of it and took a gelding—on account of them wild stallions. They're worse'n wildcats to fight. That was— yep, five years ago, early in the spring. I got rid of Trouble that summer—"

"Before Miss Peck had her colt—before Peck was born?" Ben asked.

"Let's see—Peck's— Yes, sure. Peck's just four. He won't be five till next year," Lige said. "Say, what's the reason for all this, anyhow?"

"That's what I'd like to know?" the man in the gray suit said. "I'm interested in buying a horse."

"Look at Peck," Ben said to Lige. "Take a good look at him, Mr. Singleton. Does he look like Big Trouble? Do you see anything about him that looks like Big Trouble?"

Lige turned and looked at the brown horse. Presently he shook his head. "No, I can't say he does. Fact is, he never did. But I can see plenty of Miss Peck in him."

Gaucho nodded his head. "It's true, Ben," he said. "I see it now."

"See what?" Vince Darby demanded, unable to

contain himself any longer.

Ben turned to his father. "I believe Peck is a King colt, Pop," he said. "I thought it before I bought him. Now I'm sure. Gaucho is, too."

"But—but—" Vince said, and was too astonished to finish.

"A King colt?" Andy Blair said incredulously. "A Midnight colt? No, he can't be!"

"He looks like King, Pop," Ben said. "He looks like him. You know how it is with Keister's colts"—Keister was Vince's prized saddle-horse stallion—"you can tell every one of them."

"Yes, but—but he's registered from Big Trouble," Vince said.

Lige Singleton's brow furrowed deeply. "You mean the black stallion, that he might be Peck's daddy—that Miss Peck was maybe bred to him that time she was running out?" he said to Ben. "Well—well, I never thought of that. Well, by gum, I never thought of that. But it might be. It sure could have been—I remember now she carried her colt a long time, about a month overdue according to the way I figured, but that happens every once in a while with mares—"

"A Midnight colt," Andy Blair said, half to himself.

Then suddenly his eyes gleamed and he cried, "He *is* a Midnight colt, Ben."

"Yes, sir, I believe he is," Ben said.

"That's the breeding I've been wanting for years," Andy said.

"But there's no way of proving it," Vince said, shaking his head. "You can't prove it, Ben."

"No, sir," Ben admitted. "I just believe he is."

"Now," the man in the gray suit said, "perhaps we can get back to the reason I'm here. I understand this horse is for sale."

"Yes, sir, he is," Ben said.

"You own him, I suppose," the man said.

Ben nodded and answered, "My uncle here can give you a bill of sale for him."

"Yes, sir, I can," Uncle Wes said.

"What's the price?" the man asked.

Ben hesitated, eyed the man closely. "How much will you give?" he said presently.

Lige Singleton spoke up then. "Fifteen hundred dollars," Lige said, "that is, if you'll let me in on this. And I don't mind telling that's just twice as much as I got for him when I sold him."

"Two thousand," the man in the gray suit said.

"Three," Andy Blair said. "I bid three thousand."

"But, Andy, I didn't know you wanted him," Vince said.

"I do," Andy said, nodding his head positively.

"Three thousand and five," the other man said.

Lige Singleton sighed and said, "That let's me out. But," he went on, "I had him once."

"Four," Andy Blair said.

"Forty-two hundred and fifty," the man in the gray suit said. "That is my last bid."

"Forty-five hundred," Andy Blair said without an instant's hesitation.

"Good day, gentlemen," the man in the gray suit said and turned and walked away.

Vince Darby's eyes were fairly hanging out of their sockets. "Andy!" he said. "You can't mean it. Not forty-five hundred dollars?"

"I do," Andy Blair said and began fishing into his pocket for his checkbook. "If Ben will take it, I do. That's a Midnight colt, Vince."

"But there's no way of proving it, Mr. Blair," Ben said. "I believe he is, but his registration papers say he is out of Big Trouble."

Andy took out his fountain pen. "That doesn't

worry me at all, Ben," he said. "He's a horse I want. I saw all the proof I need back there on the track a little while ago. Who'll I make this check payable to?" He looked to Vince for the answer.

"Why, to Ben," Vince said. "It's his business."

"Ben nothing," Dixie spoke up pertly. "You make it to Ben *and Dixie* Darby."

"And," Vince said, scratching his chin, "while you're doing it, just write on there: for college educations. I don't want them using the money to buy any more race horses."

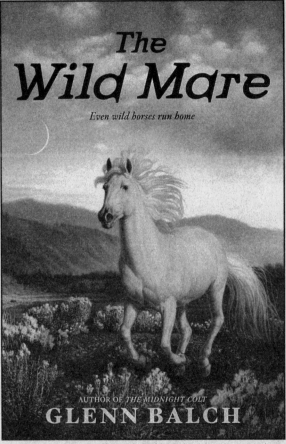